1

THE RANGER'S WIFE

By: Eveline Hart

Chapter One

Jack Walker plucked at an imagined piece of grit from his version of a U.S. Marshall uniform. He wore a pair of dark pants, boots that came to his knees which were polished to a high shine, a dark colored shirt buttoned to his neck, and a deep green vest with a dark coat laid over it. Dark was best. In fact, the lightest colored piece of clothing he owned was the green vest.

He rubbed his black gloved fingers together rapidly, a deep frown marring his normally handsome features. Of all the things he hated in the world, he was sure he hated dirt the most. He had spent even more time than normal that morning using the hot iron to create crisp creases in his pants and shirt. Today was important. His bride was coming.

Jack lifted his head, his lips a snarl, as his dark eyes watched the ship complete its position in port. He looked so angry that a woman passing by lifted her skirts so she could hurry by faster. She kept her eyes pressed down firmly towards the ground. Ever since he had received the first letter from his father with the demand that he choose a bride, he had worn that very scowl every day. Worn it like a banner. He had gone to the frontier to fight the growing wave of crime in that hostile and untamed place, but the bigger reason was to escape the tentacles of his father's imposing will. He had

7

been such a disappointment to his parents in his refusal to be groomed for the political arena which ran the East Coast. The last salvage for their tarnished reputation was to ensure a proper bride for their son to take back to the wilds he called home. He had refused, but only to himself, and had sent a letter back informing his father to just go ahead and set the whole thing up. Now he was squinting into the sunlight waiting for his mail order bride to walk down the narrow gangplank. A bride all the way from England. Were there not enough snooty women in America?

Jack sighed and ran a hand over his shoulder-length black hair. What would she think of his long hair and slim beard? Did he really care? He knew what to look for: a woman of about 5'8" with red hair and blue eyes. She would most likely be in simple dress, and as his father had described, hold an air of authority.

His father had been delighted to tell Jack that his bride to be was educated and had been raised by her successful merchant father. He also raved about her beauty.

Jack pushed his lips out but stopped himself from spitting. His father hadn't even seen the woman! How did he know what she looked like? He was given a description, and that was it. A description given by a desperate father who was worried that his daughter of twenty was becoming an old maid. Jack himself was twenty-five. So what did that make him?

In truth, she actually had been the one who picked Jack from an advertisement his father had placed. He had no doubt that some truth stretching had been used to accomplish it. She had been given a few choices by her own father, and Jack had been one of them. He had no doubts a red head with an education was going to walk down that gangplank at any moment, but he doubted she would be beautiful. He even doubted she would be slim and tall.

People were beginning their departure of the ship. Some drug their own chests, some had servants to do it for them. It wasn't hard to pick out Elizabeth Renwick from the growing throng of people. Jack felt his mouth beginning to hang open, and he closed it with an audible snap. She was, in fact, beautiful,

10

with the reddest hair peeking out from around her bonnet that he had ever seen. The bonnet suddenly was ripped backward as a strong gust coming off the water hit the disembarking passengers. The loose bun and the curls framing her face were like a beacon. Sunlight reflected off of individual hairs, and it made him think of warm fires amidst autumn foliage. She struggled with her trunk, and a rather large carpet bag while attempting to right her bonnet. He couldn't help but smile as she refused an offer from the man behind her. The man was obviously in a rush to get off the ship and rolled his eyes skyward at her polite refusal of help.

Jack pushed through the people, offering no apologies as he went up the gangplank. He yanked the chest from

Elizabeth's struggling hands and shouldered it easily. Her cry of indignation brought nothing but a grunt from him.

"Sir? Sir?" She called and followed him down to the dock, her bag tightly grasped in her hands.

Jack set the trunk down and offered his hand. "Hello."

"Thank you." She replied tartly and began another attempt at dragging the trunk. It was easier for her once it was on a flat surface.

Jack stared after her, the realization dawning that she had no idea who he was. His father must have left off all the important details, the ones he didn't like either; such as the uniform with badge and the long hair.

Jack moved forward, his 6'3" frame towering over her. Elizabeth glanced his way from the corner of her eye, her posture becoming straight and ridged.

"Thank you kindly for your assistance, but I'm here to meet my husband. My soon to be husband, that is."

Jack worked his mouth, his eyes steady. "Are you Elizabeth Renwick?"

Her brow drew together, her full lips puckered in a frown. "Yes. How..." Her eyes grew wide.

Jack extended his hand to her once more. "I'm Jack Walker."

She looked him up and down before taking his hand lightly, letting it go as soon as possible. She eyed the badge he normally wore on his vest but had transferred that morning to the outside of his jacket.

"You're a constable?"

Jack liked her accent. It was soothing, carried by a low silky voice.

"No. Not a constable. I'm a U.S. Marshall."

"I see." It was obvious she was disappointed. Jack had a sinking feeling she was disappointed in more than just his uniform. She eyed his beard and hair critically but said nothing.

"I have a room for us," Jack said and shouldered the trunk again.

"A room…as in a single room?" She shook her head and began to follow him, her gray skirt hiked to just above her ankle. "Sir, we cannot stay in a room together until after we have been married!"

"Well, unfortunately, there isn't time to set things up with a minister."

"Priest." She corrected.

"Right." He glanced at her, already growing irritated. "Anyway. The caravan I have to help secure leaves first thing in the morning. The hotel where we are all staying is booked up."

"I didn't realize we would be traveling right away." She pushed loose strands of hair back under her fancy bonnet and sighed audibly. "I also didn't realize we were traveling with a group."

"I'm sorry to disappoint you." He replied dryly. "This trip is part work, and…" He glanced at her uneasily. "Part pleasure."

"Be that as it may, we simply cannot reside in the same room tonight." She lifted her chin as she hurried to keep up with him, her small feet needing to take three steps for each of his one.

"Believe me; we will be safer in a group anyway. Indians are still an occasional problem, and there is a gang of thieves wreaking havoc from here to Maine."

"Thieves…"

Jack almost laughed out loud as he glanced back at her blanched face.

"They didn't have thieves in England?"

16

Elizabeth blinked and stepped up onto a wooden walkway. "I suppose so." She gave her head a little shake. "I know so, but I wasn't directly affected by any."

"Here we are." Jack said and opened the doors of a simple hotel called 'Thompsons'.

Elizabeth followed him in, looking around with a mild form of distaste. The hotel had a large dining area, complete with bar, which seemed to take up at least half of the first floor. The other half was a sitting area. Several men looked up from their newspapers and brandies as Jack sauntered across the patterned rug and headed for the stairs.

"Don't we have to check in?"

"No. I already took care of the room."

Elizabeth lowered her eyes as one of the men, a handsome man with a thin mustache, watched her appreciatively, with an open curiosity concerning Jack. She was used to the attentions of men but often thought it crass the way they openly stared. Had none of them heard the words of Jesus concerning looking upon a woman lustfully?

Elizabeth followed Jack up the stairs and to their room. She was about to voice more of a protest about sharing the room when he opened the door and set her trunk on the floor. He had hung twine across the room and a wool blanket separated a bed from a deep gold chaise lounge.

"I had to pay a little extra for the sofa, but I wanted this to be as proper as I could make it."

Elizabeth appreciated the gesture, but it would hardly do. Unfortunately, she would have to make it do.

"Thank you, Mr. Walker."

"You can call me Jack. Our situation doesn't call for formality now does it?"

"I suppose not." She cleared her throat. "You may call me Piper."

"Piper?"

"Yes. It's the nickname my father gave me when I was a child."

"Piper," he repeated, allowing the word to roll off his tongue. He liked it. It was the type of nickname someone would give a spirited hearty child. He hoped she would be both as a grown woman. She would need to be.

"Are you hungry? I already paid for meals for us for the night."

Piper raised her eyebrows. He certainly had tried to think of everything. "I need to freshen up and perhaps take a short nap." She forced a small smile. "I still have my sea legs about me."

Jack nodded. "Sure. You go ahead and do that. I'll come back in a couple hours and get you for supper."

Piper nodded her head. She remained standing still, staring at the door for a long moment after he had left. The sting of tears threatened her eyesight, but she pushed them back, squaring her shoulders and lifting her chin.

She set her drawstring purse on the bed and opened her small carpet bag, pulling her worn Bible from the contents.

"Father God. Is this truly what you have portioned for me?" She whispered and sat on the edge of the bed. Her solace since she was a small child, since she had been left without a mother, had been God's holy word. It was still her solace. At times her only solace.

"Please show me how to handle this." A small tear leaked from the corner of her eyes, escaping the rigid strength she had honed with a prideful persistence. She sniffed once and wiped it away, flicking her fingers as if the wetness was an annoying bug, and opened her Bible to the Psalms.

Jack stepped to the bar and slid his eyes to his old friend and mentor, Benjamin Graves. His cowboy hat was pushed back on his head revealing his brown hair with gray speckled through it. His beard was the same, and a bit untidy.

"Hope you're going to clean up before we leave tomorrow."

"What for? We're riding into the wilds. Who cares?"

"You used to always care. We need to present ourselves as the authority that we are."

Benjamin licked his lips and signaled the bartender.

"My friend here will enjoy what I partake of." Benjamin gave the bartender a wide grin. "Make it a double. He suffers from a deplorable case of stuffiness."

"You've been reading that Dicken's fellow again, haven't you?" Jack asked as he nodded to the bartender.

"A tad."

"Great maybe you and my bride will have a lot to talk about." He said dryly.

Benjamin turned his head and studied his friend's profile as he sent the double shot of liquid fire down the back of his throat. He admired the way Jack barely winced.

"Is she everything your father had said she was?"

"She's beautiful. I will give him his truth on that one, but I suspect she will be a handful."

"Why?"

Jack shrugged, shaking his head as the bartender tried to refill his glass.

"She seems used to…"

"Servants?"

"No. More like, she seems used to being in control."

"Ah. Well, a strong woman will be good. She can't be weak."

"No, but I need one who will listen to me."

"So, set some rules."

Jack rubbed the back of his neck. "I will. After we leave. I don't want her hightailing it back to the docks to wait for the next ship back to England. My father would have a fit."

Benjamin laughed heartily. "I doubt she came all this way just to run off the minute you set a few rules. Most will be for her own safety anyway."

"Any word on the Faceless Gang?" Jack asked, happy to change the subject.

"No. I went over to the jail and tried to speak with some of the lawmen, but they have their heads stuck where the sun doesn't shine. Talking about how equipped they are."

25

Jack blew air from his nose. "I hope Detroit doesn't grow into the snobby city this one has."

"Me too."

"I tried to explain that the gang hit a train coming from New York to Boston already. They just laughed it off. Said that was not under the jurisdiction of Boston, and the train line should be more careful." He grimaced over his last words. "Cocky. They had the nerve to say that I should be out there doing my job."

Jack grinned. His friend was known for his temper. "And how did you respond?

"I'd rather not repeat it."

Jack talked with Benjamin for another hour before wandering outside to check the final travel arrangements for the horses and wagons. Five covered wagons, one uncovered, and twenty horse's total, counting the ones pulling the wagons. And there was also some fancy buggy that he was sure wouldn't make the trip. It was a small caravan by western standards, but this wasn't men and their families going to claim land or cash in on the growing gold fever. This was men and their families who were under the siren's call for money and power. Most were bankers, but a few business men were in the mix. One such man hoped to open a textile company once he reached Detroit. Unlike Boston, Detroit was an up and coming city. Boston held obstacles for this particular group of men. The main one being old money and an established network of power surrounding said old money. Jack would be happy to be rid of Boston. He wanted to breathe the heady air of the wilderness and look out over rolling hills to see distant mountains. Even he despised the fact that his Marshall base was a 'city', but it wouldn't have to be forever. His hopes were to one day have a farm near Detroit. A farm that he and his wife could build together. Thankfully his mother and father were secure in Williamsburg and nowhere near to meet and influence his soon to be wife.

Jack grimaced as he walked back to the hotel. He didn't quite think Piper was going to like his plan for the future. She certainly was simpler in manner and dress than he had expected, but that didn't mean she was cut out for life as a farmer's wife. Besides, Jack knew he had his own siren's call to deal with. Giving up chasing the bad guys might not be as easy as just saying it. It worked like a drug for Jack. Nothing pushed his senses quite like the chase. Was Piper cut out for that kind of life? A life of worry whether or not her husband would return every time he had to leave?

Jack took to the stairs and hesitated when he came to the room he shared with Piper. Should he knock? It was unfortunate that the door opened to reveal more of her side than his. He sorely wished it was the other way around. To be safe, he rapped on the door twice and counted to three before he entered. His eyes widened in surprise when he ran into Piper as soon as the door opened. She stared up at him blankly.

"I was coming to answer the door."

"Oh."

"Did you need something? You don't have to knock, you know. This is your room too."

"I didn't want to catch you…ah…unawares."

"I see." She folded her hands primly in front of her. "That's kind of you."

"Are you ready for supper?"

"I assume that's the same as dinner?"

Jack bit back his words to the point that his tongue hurt. "Yes, Ma'am, it is."

"Then yes, I am ready." She walked past him and through the still open door.

Jack raised his eyes to the ceiling. Please give me strength.

Dinner was spent in near silence. Piper was looking around herself most of the time with nervous and, at times, judging eyes. Jack could only imagine what she was used to in England. It apparently wasn't anything like Boston.

"You don't have any disrespect for me since I'm American do you?"

Piper slid her clear blue eyes to his much darker brown ones. "Now, why would you ask such a foolish thing?"

Jack could feel heat rising past his collar. "Well, you know...the war and all."

"Which has been officially over for seventy-two years."

"Yes, that's true, but..."

Her face was like stone. "Are you implying that all of the Brits are grudge holding narrow-minded people?"

Jack's eyes bulged from their sockets. "No, Ma'am!"

"Please stop calling me that. Call me Piper."

"Alright. And I was only asking because you seem a little bit...well...disgusted by the people here."

"I find some of the snippets of conversation I'm over hearing vulgar, and some of these people could use a bath, but other than that, it doesn't look much different than some of the hotels I've seen in Great Britain." She sipped at her spoon, taking a tiny portion of soup into her mouth. "A few places I have seen were downright shameless."

Jack grinned. "And how did you find yourself in such a place?"

"I do missionary work. Three other women and I would bring clothes and sometimes medical help for some of the poor women and their children." Her eyes lowered. "Most of them were prostitutes. We also brought them the word of God."

Jack was rendered speechless. He had a hard time wrapping his mind around the prim and proper woman seated across from him as having the gumption, and more importantly the desire, to enter a whore house.

"That's really something else. You should be very proud to have done work like that."

"Let nothing be done through strife or vainglory, but in lowliness of mind let each esteem others better than themselves."

Jack blinked. "Huh?"

"The book of Philippians. That's where that verse can be found."

"Oh...the Bible."

She looked at him sharply. "Yes, the Bible. Are you not a Christian? My father assured me you were."

34

"I mean, I do believe in God. I attend church on all the major holidays."

Piper pursed her lips. "I will attend church every Sunday. I expect my husband to do the same."

Jack had reached the sudden end of his rope. He leaned forward to tell her exactly what she could do with what she expected when Benjamin approached the table.

"Evening folks." Benjamin smiled, his eyes lighting on Piper.

"Piper, this is my friend and fellow Marshall Benjamin Graves."

Benjamin removed his hat and nodded to Piper. "Pleasure to meet you. Ma'am."

"You as well." She smiled pleasantly. "Will you be traveling with us to Detroit?"

"Yes, Ma'am, I will."

"Please…would you like to join us?"

Jack shifted his eyes to Piper. He wasn't sure he wanted a third person at the already cramped table, but maybe the distraction would be good for them both.

"No, thank you, Ma'am. I'm sure I'll have plenty of time for visiting once the caravan leaves."

"Not really," Jack commented. "We'll have our hands full."

Benjamin clamped a hand on his shoulder. It felt more like a warning than a friendly gesture.

"Aww, now; we can't have all work and no play." He winked at Piper and gave her a nod. "Nice meeting you, Piper."

"You as well." She replied, the note of disappointment in her voice unmistakable.

Guess I'm not good enough company.

They ate in relative silence, and Jack soon found himself back up in their makeshift dual room. He lit two candles, handing one to Piper. Her slim finger slipped through the finger hole and the rest of her hand wrapped around the base of the candle holder.

"Thank you."

"Goodnight."

Piper watched him round the edge of the hanging blanket. His large frame was, at times, graceful; poetic even. Still, he wasn't at all what she would have picked for herself.

"Goodnight," Piper called after him.

She took off as little as possible to be able to sleep comfortably. She had no doubt that Jack's intentions were pure. Why else would he have gone to all the trouble of making the room separate? She was worried less about him than the other patrons of the hotel.

Light vanished from Jack's side of the blanket, and Piper mouthed silent prayers to God for mercy, blessing, and patience. The moment she blew out her own candle a sound rumbled through the room. It was a soft rumble that soon became a distinctive sawing noise. She risked a peek around the hanging blanket and saw Jack laying on his back, his gun belt laying at his feet, and his boots neatly side by side on the floor. The sound was emanating from his open mouth.

Piper slipped back to her bed and laid down. She stared at the darkened ceiling, a grimace deeply etched on her pretty face.

"Lord Jesus, help me. The man snores!"

Chapter Two

Jack looked at Piper sitting listlessly on the edge of the bed, her eyes tainted with dark circles beneath. He frowned and hoped they wouldn't require a trip to the doctor before departing. The sun had just crested the horizon, and they needed to be on their way.

"Are you ill?"

She turned her head slowly. "Ill?"

"Yes, Ma'am."

"No. I'm tired." Her head came forward, and her eyes stared at him intensely.

Jack's brow came together. "You couldn't sleep last night?"

"Oh, I tried, but your infernal snoring kept me up all night!" She stood abruptly and plopped a bonnet on her head, tying the wide matching ribbon under her chin with deft fingers, leaving a bow to rest under the right side of her jaw. Jack didn't think it would be wise to tell her that she looked cute as a button. The lace around the sides and top of the headwear framed her face perfectly, and the plain green of the rest of her bonnet complimented her dress. But no, now was not the time for compliments. It was the time for apologies.

"I'm sorry. I can't exactly help it."

"Laying on your side will help it." She replied, slipping green gloves over her hands.

"I'll keep that in mind," Jack replied dryly, wondering how she knew he slept on his back. Curiosity must have gotten the better of her. He liked the thought of her peeking around the blanket at him while he slept. A smile crept over his lips, spreading the sides of his thin beard. One look at Piper's irritated face swept his good humor away.

"I'll take you down for breakfast, but I need to load your things onto the wagon you will be occupying, and there are a few other things for me to tend to."

"Where are your things at?"

"Saddlebag." He pointed towards the corner of the room.

Piper's expression told him she didn't approve of 'things' being kept in a dusty saddle bag. Jack wanted to explain that it was worn and that he kept it as clean as his clothes, but he refrained. The woman just seemed too critical on all accounts, and he preferred to not have unnecessary arguments. He saved his vigor and heat for the outlaws.

"I can see to my own breakfast. Thank you." Piper said politely, but Jack could still feel a chill as she exited the room. He turned his face upward for a moment and asked the Creator for help understanding his most complicated of creatures.

Piper stood primly next to the covered wagon Jack indicated she would be riding in for most of the journey. It would hold the Brackett family. A plump woman with frizzy red hair, pinned as neatly as she could make it under her bonnet, smiled warmly at Piper. Four children would also share the wagon, three of which were boys that resembled stair steps when standing in a row. Piper had watched with increasing eye size as Bonnie placed a hand on each boy's head in the way of introduction.

"Thomas. He's eleven. Timothy. He's ten. Tyler. He's eight. And this is Ruth. She's eleven months." Bonnie smiled down at the little girl who was clinging to her mother's hip and side. She gave Piper a shy slide of the eye before smiling dramatically, revealing two teeth in the bottom of her mouth.

"They are…" Piper began. "They are just beautiful children." She smiled in what she hoped was a warm manner. She loved children, she really did, but the line of little boys had mischievous smiles beneath their various shades of red hair. All of the children certainly took after their mother in the looks department. Only the baby resembled her father by way of her blue eyes and pale hair.

"Now, don't worry about them. I'll make sure they mind their manners." Bonnie Brackett assured her. She seemed greatly relieved to see an extra woman along for the journey.

Benjamin Graves trotted past them on his gelding and tipped his hat.

"We're about ready to leave, ladies."

Piper smiled benignly to him while fighting the urge to double over from nervous stomach cramping.

This is it, Lord. My new unwanted life is about to begin. Please grant me patience.

"May I help you up?" Jack was beside her before she realized he was. He held out a black-clad hand to her, but his face didn't show any emotion. She wondered what was going on behind his dark brown eyes. Was he nervous too? Piper barely shook her head at the thought. The man was a U.S.

Marshall. He probably hadn't been nervous a day in his life.

"Thank you," Piper said and stepped up into the back of the wagon, taking a seat beside Bonnie, and smoothing her skirts in one movement.

Jack tipped his hat and wandered a few feet away to speak to Mr. Brackett. Bonnie leaned her head close.

"He's going to be your husband?"

Piper nodded feebly. "Yes."

"Oh my, but aren't you the lucky one! He's very handsome!" She whispered.

Piper stared at Jack's profile, her brow drawn inward. Handsome? She tried to see what her riding companion saw. Yes, she supposed he was handsome, but that beard! It made him look grizzled and unkempt, even if it was tidily shaven down. At least the hair was pulled back in a neat ponytail for the trip.

Bonnie settled Ruth on her lap and exhaled sharply.

"I hope we don't run into any Indians."

Piper turned her head and studied Bonnie's profile.

"Indians?"

"Yes. We will have to go through New York and Ohio to get to Detroit, and there are still a few Shawnee scattered about." She shrugged in a far more casual manner than Piper cared for. "Iroquois too." She shook her head. "There's more Indian tribes than we can shake a stick at."

48

"I guess I should have educated myself more properly concerning them."

Bonnie let out a light laugh.

"You are far too young to have had time for that! A person could study them for a lifetime and still not have an understanding of their ways and languages."

Piper needed to choose her words carefully. This was no time to offend her wagon mate. They hadn't even left yet.

"The good book says that we are to love our neighbor. They are like our neighbors, yes?"

Bonnie looked at Piper with a simultaneous critical yet patient eye.

"Your accent tells me you didn't grow up here."

"No, I didn't. I just arrived yesterday. I grew up in England."

The statement did little to appease Bonnie. Her eyes held a harder glint after the word 'England'.

"The Indians are too hard to manage. They attack, steal women, and steal anything else they can get their hands on."

"Like the way the British and French came and stole their land?"

Bonnie's face went completely blank.

"Stole their land?"

"Yes. The Indians lived here first, did they not?"

Bonnie looked at each of her children as they watched the conversation play out.

"I...I hadn't thought of it that way before." A shadow crossed her face. "I guess maybe that was why so many behaved so badly."

"That's a good assumption." Piper felt sorry for the woman. She assumed most of the Americans were under the same assumption that the Indian land was something owed to them. Piper resolved to speak to Jack about the current situation. She cast a look out of the back of the wagon. He mounted his reddish brown horse and called out an order for everyone to mount up or enter their wagons. Maybe Jack wouldn't be the right person to ask. She had no doubt that all of his sympathies would lie with his own people. She needed an unbiased person to educate her.

"Thomas! Stop that!" Bonnie had already moved on from talk about the Indians to trying to keep her boys in line.

The wagon began to move, and Piper called up a silent prayer for strength, patience, and right words. She had a feeling she would offer up many silent prayers in the weeks to come.

The wagon train stopped two hours into their journey to give the party a rest from riding, whether it was in the back of a wagon or on horseback. Jack and Benjamin had found a beautiful open field between towns with several heavily shaded trees; their bright green leaves told the world that spring had indeed sprung.

Piper watched Jack move amongst the people, answering questions and checking all of the wheels on the wagons. He was a quiet, yet brusque man. He was a mystery. That would never do if they were to be man and wife. She needed a fresh perspective on her soon to be husband.

Piper allowed her eyes to scan the cluster of wagons and horses. When her blue eyes landed on Benjamin Graves, she knew he was the one person available who could shine some light on this mysterious man Jack Walker.

Piper lifted her skirts and began picking her way over the uneven grass of the field. Benjamin was tending to his horse and stopped to pull something out of his saddlebag wrapped in cheese cloth.

"Hello," Piper said and hoped it sounded cheery.

Benjamin turned his head, and his face opened with a smile.

"Hello there, Piper. Is everything alright?"

"Yes," she nodded and folded her hands neatly over her skirts. "I wanted to ask you a few questions."

"Sure." He held out the open cheese cloth and held it towards her. "Would you like some?"

Piper looked at the rough bread and block of cheese.

"Oh, no thank you. I wanted to talk to you about Jack, actually."

He nodded knowingly and motioned for her to come sit under the tree.

"Getting a little nervous about marrying a complete stranger?"

Piper took his hand as he helped her lower herself to the ground. She spread her skirts and cursed the need to wear a cage that kept her skirts from tangling about her legs.

"It is a daunting task ahead of me." She agreed.

Benjamin laughed heartily as he ripped a piece of the bread loose and did the same with the cheese.

"Well, what would you like to know?"

Piper blinked. What would she like to know? She ran a hand along the edge of her bonnet, making sure her hair was still in place beneath it.

"I think…everything."

"Black Hands looks like a hard puzzle from the outside, but he really is a simple man on the inside."

"Black Hands?"

He nodded. "It's his nickname. You know…because he wears those infernal black gloves everywhere he goes."

"I see. And why does he do that?"

Benjamin leaned towards her as if he were about to impart a spectacular secret.

"He has a problem with dirt."

"Dirt," she replied flatly.

"You ever seen a U.S. Marshall with clothes that clean before?"

"Mr. Graves, before yesterday, I hadn't seen a U.S. Marshall period." She smiled kindly.

"That's true," he agreed and popped the cheese and bread into his mouth. Much to her surprise he actually chewed and swallowed before continuing the conversation. "He hates to be dirty. And I do mean hates. Sometimes we have to get rough with the outlaws, and he'll gladly do it, but afterward he's miserable until his clothes can be laundered and his body too for that matter."

Piper moved her eyes across the field. Jack was standing near his horse, brushing himself off. It suddenly made sense as to why he was constantly inspecting his clothing, and touching his beard. She had thought him vain. Now she knew better.

"As far as the rest of Jack, well…it's pretty easy. Before he announced that you were coming, he was married to his work. He's twenty-five and lives like he's fifty-five sometimes."

Piper lowered her head. Twenty-five?

"I would have thought him at least thirty," she sighed. "That's it, is it?"

Benjamin nodded. "Pretty much."

"What are his interests?"

"Criminals."

"His hobbies?"

"Criminals."

Piper was becoming irritated.

"His hopes and dreams? And please do not say criminals!"

Benjamin threw his head back and laughed.

"No, sweetheart, not criminals. He really just wants a little farm."

Piper felt her chest contract with disappointment. A humble little farmer. No aspirations for anything greater.

"Stealing her from me already, Ben?" Jack said smoothly. He stood before them with a hip cocked easily to the side and his hands resting lightly on his hips. From the angle and lighting, he was an impressive, handsome sight. Piper felt a quickening of her heart but immediately admonished herself for it. It had just been a trick of the eye.

"We were just talking about you," Benjamin said with a grin.

"I bet you were." Jack looked down at Piper. "I have some lunch for us if you would like to have it."

Piper raised her hand, and Jack took it, gently pulling her to her feet.

"Cheese and bread?"

"Those things yes, but I also have some dried meat and an apple we can share."

"Yes, I am a bit hungry." Piper turned to Benjamin. "Thank you for the conversation."

"Anytime, Ma'am," he replied and laughed lightly as Jack gave him a dark look over his shoulder.

The second leg of the first day was the hardest. Jack pushed for the wagon train to continue on, the next stop being for the night. They entered a hamlet southwest of Boston, a little place where farms dotted the countryside and wooded areas with a single dirt street centered as the hamlet's town proper.

With a frown puckering her lips and her hands planted on her slim waist, Piper surveyed the scant accommodations offered. A restaurant/saloon/inn called the Bridle and Hook was the only place to stay other than the wagons. Its sign, in much need of touch up paint on the splintered wood, moved lazily on its chains in the breeze. There was a church at the end of the street, a doctor's office across from the Bridle and Hook, and something that she assumed was a mercantile store of some sort. The simple letters painted on the glass announced that it was just 'General'. General what?

"Not much to see is there?" a smooth voice said beside her. Piper turned her head and looked up at the smiling face of a man who had blonde hair neatly combed to the side. His hat was already in his hands. Piper flicked her eyes hastily over his dark checkered pants with matching jacket. A vest of matching color to the pale checkering was visible along his flat stomach. He was obviously a man of taste and most likely money.

"No, not really," Piper replied.

"I'm Charles Dewitt." His green eyes seemed to sparkle as he bowed slightly with an arm over his chest.

"Elizabeth Renwick." She offered her hand, a ghost of a smile moving her features as he bent again, pressing his lips momentarily to her gloved knuckles. "Everyone calls me Piper."

Charles straightened and continued smiling at her.

"Are you traveling alone?"

"I'm..." She blinked. "No. I actually am officially traveling with Jack Walker."

Charles's face underwent a subtle change which he quickly recovered from.

"The Marshall?"

"The very one," Piper replied dryly.

"Are you in trouble?"

"No! He's...we...we're promised," she finished hastily, the words burning her tongue.

"Ah," he nodded his understanding. "Let me guess, you came across the ocean because your marriage was arranged?"

"Not exactly, I chose him from an advertisement my father presented to me. How did you know I came across the ocean? I could have been born here." She was feeling flirtatious all of a sudden and couldn't help but look up at him with a teasing smile.

"Not with an accent that strong you weren't."

"That obvious is it?"

"It is, but it makes your voice all the more beautiful."

Piper felt a blush creep along her cheeks.

"And what of yourself, Mr. Dewitt? Are you traveling with anyone?"

"No, Ma'am. I'm heading to Detroit to cash in on all the hoopla."

"You're a business man then?"

"I am." He said proudly. "I'm going to open my own establishment like this poor example here." He moved his arm in a careless gesture towards the Bridle and Hook. "But mine will not be a poor example. It will be fine with lots of brass and velvet."

"You've already owned a business like it before?"

"No, but I know that's what I would like to do."

Piper considered his words. He had a definite plan. A dream. It sounded better than settling on being a simple farmer.

"I wish you the best of luck, Mr. Dewitt." Piper smiled and wrapped her shawl tighter against the cooling air of the dying sunlight.

Charles placed his hat back on his head and bowed again.

"Thank you, and please, call me Charles. I hope we can talk again." He moved away from her, and Piper was struck by his graceful way. He was a gentleman if she had ever seen one.

Now, why couldn't that have been the man father sent me too?

Chapter Three

"Sir, a dollar and a half a piece for us to stay is robbery." Piper's face was burning with indignation. "The only ones who will be staying indoors will be the women and girl children. My goodness, but we could share space and only occupy three of your rooms! Now, I demand you give us a fair price for rooms, not an outrageous one based on head count!"

Benjamin nudged Jack in the ribs, his smile and nod towards Piper's back indicative of being impressed.

Jack had a hand wrapped around his chin. He had to admit; Piper was a shrewd and tough business minded woman.

The owner of the Bridle and Hook ran a hand over his balding gray head. He looked like he wanted to spit on his own floor.

"Now look, Missy. Times are hard! I have to run a business!"

"How many rooms are available?"

"All of them, but…"

"All of them?"

"Yes." He replied sheepishly.

"So, if the women decide to stay in the elements and not in here; you very well stand to not make a dime on the rooms all night."

"Possibly." He reluctantly agreed, his watery eyes already showing defeat.

Piper swallowed and stared at him for a moment.

"Alright, Mr. Bledsoe. The women will agree to strip the beds in the morning instead of you or your chamber maid. What is your cost per room?"

"A dollar and a quarter with no meal. Three dollars for dinner and breakfast to be included." He shook his head. "No need to change the bed things."

"Thank you, Mr. Bledsoe," Piper beamed. "You have very reasonable prices." The compliment seemed to soothe him, and Piper continued on. "Would there be a possible deal for say, several loaves of bread and some cheese for our journey once we leave in the morning?"

Mr. Bledsoe regarded her blankly, with a twitch developing below his left eye.

"Perhaps for an extra fifty cents per room?" Piper prompted.

Mr. Bledsoe shook his head. "You, Miss, have a talent for bartering." He ran a hand along the side of his face. "Alright. One loaf and a quarter pound of cheese per room."

Piper thanked him and turned to address Jack directly. "He has eight rooms. I don't see why the married men should be away from their families."

"You can share a room with us," Bonnie said.

71

Piper plastered the most sincere smile she could on her face. She didn't want to hurt her feelings, but Piper desperately needed a break from Bonnie's children. Poor Bonnie herself had become the likes of a person suffering from multiple personalities. One minute she was happy and chatting, the next roaring at the children to 'Stop' or 'Get right over here.'

"That is very sweet, but I think I will just get a room of my own or something. The McKenzie's have three daughters, I could share with a couple of them."

"I guess it would be a tight fit," Bonnie agreed.

"Yes, but it was a kind offer." Piper touched her arm before Bonnie wandered away, Ruth snug on her hip.

Jack opened his mouth to offer a compliment for what he had just witnessed Piper accomplish with the inn keep, but snapped it shut as he watched a man begin weaving his way towards Piper's back. His jacket and vest carried the look of someone who had been traveling for a long time without benefit of a bath.

"How much?" The man raised his voice just behind Piper. She turned abruptly and looked at the man sharply, before allowing her eyes to wander over him in disgust.

"How much for what?"

He grinned, stretching his unshaven cheeks to reveal a mouth void of half of its teeth.

"For you!"

"I beg your pardon?" Piper replied, her voice rising in pitch and her eyebrows shooting upward.

"Aww, come on…no need to be shy about it!" He reached forward and grabbed Piper at her waist, attempting to pull her towards himself.

"Take your hands off of her!" Jack growled.

"Wait yer turn!" The man didn't have time to blink before Jack's fist caught him under the chin. He staggered backward into a chair, his head lolling as he fell unconscious.

Piper looked at Jack with wide eyes.

"I'll not have any trouble here!" Mr. Bledsoe called, hurrying back to them. "You want trouble? Stay in your wagons!"

Piper raised her hands and shook her head. "No, there's not going to be trouble." She shot Jack a warning look, glad to see Benjamin had him by the crook of the arm, the fist at the end still clenched. "There won't be any trouble. Right, Jack?"

Jack noted the fading zing of how good it felt to knock the drunk man cold.

"Better not be," Mr. Bledsoe said with a raised chin before leaving them alone once again.

Piper's chest rose. She had a mouthful for Jack Walker, but a gentle hand at her waist kept her silent. She looked up into the bright green worried eyes of Charles Dewitt.

"Come Piper. Let's get you to a quiet place in here away from the riff raff." He gave Jack a pointed look while easily leading Piper away.

"He's going to be next," Jack breathed, snatching his arm away from Benjamin.

Benjamin leaned in and spoke to him quietly.

"Don't forget the office you represent."

Jack turned his head and allowed Benjamin to see the darkness smoldering in his deep brown eyes.

"That man thought she was a prostitute!"

"I know, Jack, but…"

"And that other one thinks…well, I don't rightly know what he's thinking!"

Benjamin nodded, his lips forming a straight line.

"She isn't married to you yet. Just keep an eye on it. Don't make me regret agreeing to this situation." Benjamin clasped Jack's shoulder and walked away.

Jack ignored the looks of the remaining patrons of the Bridle and Hook, his face turned to a snug corner of the large room where Piper sat with Charles Dewitt and two other men. She turned her face to him, her displeasure evident. Jack sighed. Her displeasure wasn't with her current company. It was with him.

How am I going to court a fiancée while I'm protecting a wagon train?

He cast a final look at her, another sigh escaping, as her face turned back to Charles Dewitt. A smile spread on her beautiful face at something he had whispered to her. Much to Jack's chagrin, the smile was preceded by a shy lowering of her eyes and a sweet blush.

Chapter Four

The next morning dawned gray and the air smelled of impending rain. Piper looked out through the doorway of the Bridle and Hook, her thoughts on muddy roads and wagon wheels sinking to a wagon's axle.

Jack looked up from saddling his horse and watched Piper for a moment. She seemed lost in whatever thoughts she was having, her fair skin creased across her forehead. He moved towards the doorway of the inn without her even being aware that he was there.

"What's troubling you?" His voice was soft, gentler than he had spoken for a long time.

Piper shook her head slightly and turned her face up to him.

"I worry about rain."

Jack laughed lightly, one side of his mouth raising, but his eyes were kind.

"You're afraid we'll get stuck?"

Piper nodded.

"I've escorted a few caravans. Believe me, this route is easier than some of the others I've been on. I won't let any of the wagons get stuck."

"Some are weighed down by quite a bit."

Jack angled his head closer to hers to avoid nosey ears.

"Yes, especially the one you ride in. Bonnie has what? Fourteen children?"

Piper couldn't help but smile. His attempt at levity wiped away some of her worries.

"Not quite fourteen." Her smile faded. "Tell me about the Indians we may encounter."

"We'll keep a watch out. The Indian population is thin right now. Soon there won't even be a population to count, I'm afraid."

Piper lowered her eyes. It was a topic she and Bonnie had touched on, and it seemed to enter her mind every few hours. She didn't like being conflicted. She believed

in resolve and sticking to principles. How
could one pick a principle in this situation?
She lifted her eyes again to see Jack staring
at her intently, waiting for her next statement.
It was an odd sensation. Her father would
have already busied himself with something
else, and she would have to interrupt him
again to get his attention, but Jack was
waiting on her.

"You don't entirely agree with their
removal, do you?"

Jack sighed lightly. He opened his
mouth and shut it again right away.

"What is it?"

"Sometimes it's hard to be a Marshall. I
believe in the opportunity this country offers.
I just...I just know we take it for granted."

"Hey, Jack?" Benjamin called, drawing Jack's attention from Piper. Jack turned and nodded, but returned his attention back to Piper before stepping away.

"I have to see what he wants. Excuse me." He tipped his hat and walked away.

Piper watched him with a new sense of curiosity. She had no idea who this man Jack Walker was, but she was determined to find out. How could she give him a fair shake if she didn't even get to know him? Piper resolved to walk with him during one of the slow downs, or perhaps to eat lunch with him.

Piper turned on her heel and went in search of Mr. Bledsoe. There was a matter to be settled concerning staples for the next leg of the journey.

"I'm going to drive Mr. Baxter's wagon for a bit," Jack announced as they gathered their things from the first rest of the day. "We'll be crossing into New York before tomorrow's nightfall."

"What's wrong with Mr. Baxter?" Piper asked, conjuring an image of the gray-haired businessman and his equally gray-haired wife.

"He's not feeling well. His wife said she thinks he's feverish."

"And your horse?"

"Easy fix. We'll just tie him to the back. No problem. He'll keep up."

Piper cleared her throat, grateful for the opportunity she had been afforded.

"If you don't mind, I would like to ride with you."

Jack stared at her blankly. She wanted to ride with him?

Piper's chin raised a fraction, her pride already bruised.

"If that isn't convenient for you then..."

"Oh no!" Jack countered, his eyes large. "I'm fine with it. I would like it, actually. I'm just surprised."

Piper smoothed her skirt with moist nervous hands.

"Well, we have to get to know each other sometime, don't we?"

Jack nodded. "Yes, Ma'am, I think it's a good idea to do that."

"I'll let Bonnie know, and then we can be on our way."

Jack watched his future wife walk away with determined steps, growling lightly as Charles Dewitt rode up beside her and stopped her progress. He wished he could hear what was being said, but apparently, his name was brought up judging from the way Piper motioned behind herself in his general direction. Jack met the swift look they both gave him with what he was sure looked like a scowl. Sometimes he wished he could iron his face flat. Soon she waved cheerily and continued on to the wagon she shared with Bonnie and her riotous family. Jack didn't have to wonder why Blaine Brackett always looked so tired.

Jack waited at the wagon side. They would be lead, and that was all right with him. Seeing the country open around them, and having an opportunity to sit with Piper gave him a happy feeling. He couldn't recognize it at first. Real happiness had eluded him for a long time. He always seemed to just be, without actually living. He enjoyed the chase. He enjoyed bringing criminals to justice, but they were temporary fixes. He guessed he was just plain lonely. Now there was a chance before him to balm that loneliness.

If I can just keep Charles Dewitt's grubby hands off of her!

Jack reminded himself to keep his face calm and to not mash it all up in angry expressions, as Charles rode his horse slowly beside Piper's returning frame. He dismounted and held a hand out to Piper. She smiled warmly and allowed him to help her up onto the wagon seat.

I was supposed to do that.

Charles swung himself back into the saddle and looked at Jack over the backs of the horses. They stamped their feet eager to be moving again.

"Marshall," Charles commented and rode to the back of the caravan, a smug expression on his face.

Jack stepped up into the wagon and took the seat next to Piper. Her hands were folded primly on her lap, almost invisible as they were nearly swallowed up by the dark gloves and deep blue of her dress. She seemed to have plenty of clothes, but they were all relatively simple and void of a lot of decoration. He liked that. He liked a humble woman.

"Ready?"

"Yes," Piper replied, but her eyes had an energy which kept them roving.

Jack moved the wooden brake with his hand and grasped the reins with both hands, snapping his wrists and letting out a low whistle. The horses began moving immediately.

"Is Mr. Baxter in the back?"

"Yes. His wife made a little pallet for him."

"I'll check on them once we stop."

"Good idea." Jack desperately wished that he knew more of what to say. He feared the day would draw out to be a long one. He didn't want to bore Piper. Thankfully she initiated the first conversation.

"Why did you choose to become a Marshall?"

"Lots of reasons."

Piper turned her head and gazed at his profile. She really would need to speak to him about the beard once they were husband and wife.

"Name the top three."

"Alright," he began slowly. "I love justice. I want to make a difference. I hate politics."

"What does politics have to do with it?"

"My father is a politician. It was his and my mother's dream that I follow in his footsteps." He lifted his shoulders. "I don't want the scheming and back scratching life that my father has led. He was meant for it; I wasn't."

"I understand. I was meant to be a boy." Piper smiled, laying a hand to her chest. "At least my father really wanted a boy. One who could take over his merchant businesses once he left this earth. I would have gladly done it. I spent all of my time from the point that I could talk, trying to please my father and learning all there was to know about his business. If I wasn't at his offices, I was out doing the Lord's work."

"I'm sure he's proud of you for it. For all of it."

Piper's face darkened. "No. He shipped me away to get married because that's what's proper for a lady."

Jack looked at her sharply. He didn't necessarily feel offended by what she had said, but he suddenly had a far clearer view of her situation. She had been forced to wed just as he had. At least he was able to stay where he was comfortable and around things and people he was accustomed to. She had to leave her country and travel to an entirely new place, without the benefit of knowing a soul.

"I imagine that this has been right hard on you," Jack said softly.

"Yes." Piper saw no need to embellish her words. The simple truth was always the best.

"I hope I can…" His words were cut short as a horse trotted up beside the front of the wagon. Charles Dewitt began keeping pace with them.

"Hello, Piper. Marshall."

Piper smiled warmly, but Jack only gave a nearly imperceptible nod, his lips thinning.

"Looks like the rain might hold off."

"It's only eight o'clock," Jack grumbled.

"I hope Piper will be afforded the back of a wagon if the rain does come."

"She will." Jack felt the muscles coiling along his upper back. What kind of man did he think he was? And it was none of his business!

The wagon rolled along, and Charles kept his horse steady in the silence around them.

"I do hope Detroit has a decent theatre." Charles ventured. He cut his eyes to see if Jack would respond, and when he didn't he continued on, his conversation directed at Piper.

"I saw a lovely show last fall. It was Hamlet, done so realistically, I actually felt transported back in time."

"Oh, Hamlet is one of my favorites!" Piper's eyes lit up. "I sorely wish I could have seen it. I've never seen a Shakespearian play acted out; I've only read them."

"I'll have to change that for you." Charles winked. "Theatre is part of being cultured. Wouldn't you agree, Marshall?"

Jack sighed quietly. "I haven't seen any plays either." His voice was quiet, and Piper turned her head to look at him, her smile fading.

"Well, we can't all be cultured, now can we?" Charles gave Piper a final wink before tipping his hat to her and turning his horse back to the rear of the caravan.

Piper didn't know what to say. She wanted to soothe the obvious embarrassment that Charles had caused, but at the same time, she wanted Jack to feel the embarrassment. Life couldn't always just be about catching the bad guy. There was so much more. She guessed for the moment their conversation was over.

Piper climbed from the back of the Baxter's wagon, her face flushed and her skin crawling. Whatever Mr. Baxter had was burning him up from the inside out. The older man was near to hallucinating from fever, and his skin had a shiny pulled tautness to it. Mrs. Baxter came right out after her.

"I better talk to the Marshalls," she said quietly, her gray hair coming loose from her usual bun.

"Yes," Piper agreed. "We may need to get him a doctor at our next town stop."

"It's more than just that. We carry a lot of paper money and even more gold in there!"

Piper's eyes widened considerably, and she glanced around her before pulling Mrs. Baxter further from the caravan.

"What do you mean about gold and paper money?"

"Mr. Baxter is a banker by trade. We're going to establish a bank in Detroit. Plus a few of the other people with us already banked with him, so they are having us hold some of their investment money in our wagon."

"That's why two Marshalls are escorting us?"

Mrs. Baxter nodded. "Since Jack is driving the wagon today, I felt comfortable, but I also thought my husband would bounce back from whatever this is." Her watery blue eyes searched Piper's face for some type of answer.

Piper ran a hand over her forehead. "We'll find a doctor in the next town. I'll see to it. I'll speak to Jack and Benjamin. You go ahead back to your husband."

Mrs. Baxter nodded and did as she was told. Piper helped her into the wagon before turning on her heel and searching out Jack. A hand caught her elbow gently. She looked up to see the concerned face of Charles staring down at her.

"May I help?"

"With?"

"I wasn't eavesdropping, I assure you, but I couldn't help but hear part of that conversation."

Piper tightened her jaw. "Mr. Baxter needs a doctor. I...I think we should push on until we come to a town. We've been blessed with the fact that there isn't any rain so far."

"I could ride ahead and see if there is at least a hamlet. No need to push the caravan if it's only wilderness ahead."

"Charles, that could be dangerous. You should ask Benjamin or Jack first. Maybe ask them both."

"A little danger doesn't frighten me." He smiled kindly. "Besides, I'm cautious." He opened his jacket on one side and revealed a pistol stuck in his pants at the waist. "I came prepared, just in case."

"I see," Piper commented. She was still unsure of how she felt about guns other than in a law enforcement capacity or a hunting one. She supposed carving out a new life for oneself in unfamiliar terrain required a bit of forethought and preparation concerning self-preservation. "Still. You should speak with one or both of them."

"Sure." His smile tightened. "I'll do that right now."

Piper kept her distance but soon watched as Charles Dewitt galloped away from the caravan. She followed Jack's form with a slow movement of her head as he practically stomped his way to their wagon. Was he talking to himself? He stopped and scanned the area until his eyes rested on Piper. He stared for a second too long, his face smoothing from a grimace into something Piper couldn't quite read. He lifted a gloved hand and motioned her to him.

"We're leaving." He held a hand out to her and helped her onto the bench seat of the wagon.

"Has Charles ridden ahead to look for a town?"

"Yes." Jack bit down. "I hope we don't have to waste scant manpower to form a search party for the fool." He shook his head. "I can't believe Benjamin allowed it."

"I think what he's doing is very brave," Piper sniffed.

Jack cut his eyes to her sharply but chose not to comment.

Piper willed her body to relax as the wagon began moving. She couldn't understand her mixed up mind and feelings. She had prided herself on her practicality and her lack of rashness. Yet, here she was sitting on a wagon seat beside her soon to be husband in silence, while her mind and heart went forward with the galloping hooves of Charles Dewitt's mare. He was genteel, educated, ambitious, and well spoken. Charles was everything that she had dreamed of in a husband since her youth.

Piper slid her eyes to Jack. He lacked every one of those qualities she coveted. He may very well be educated, and he wasn't badly spoken; but he was far from genteel, and he definitely wasn't ambitious. His goal was to have a little farm? No, not ambitious in the least. Yet, here he was; the man her father chose for her to marry.

But my father isn't here. If I chose one better than Jack Walker, how could he argue later?

Piper chewed on her lip as she considered her traitorous thoughts.

"What's wrong with you, woman?" Jack spit out. "Are you that worried about him?"

Piper's eyes enlarged. "I beg your pardon?"

"You're sitting over there looking practically peaked, and you may very well chew your lip right off your face!"

"I was just thinking, Jack!" she huffed loudly and crossed her arms over her chest.

"That was the ugliest thinking I have ever seen!"

Piper opened her mouth and narrowed her eyes. Had he just called her ugly?!

"Well, if that's how you feel, then stop this wagon at once and let me off! I wouldn't want you to burn your eyeballs on someone so ugly!"

Jack rolled his head from side to side. "Aww, come on, Piper. I didn't mean you were ugly! You were making a face and..."

"Stop the wagon."

Jack pulled back gently on the reins and began to slow the horses. The wagon hadn't completely stopped before Piper judged her distance and hopped off the wagon seat. She let out a small yelp as her foot landed wrong, and her ankle twisted.

"Are you alright?" Jack yelled and jumped down beside her.

"Fine." She lifted her chin and began painfully walking towards the back of the caravan. Curious eyes watched her from other wagon seats and horse backs.

With a dark stare, Jack watched her hobble away, something obviously hurting her. Benjamin began riding towards him, a question already forming on his lips.

Jack raised a hand and waved him off. "Don't ask, Ben!"

"What did you do to her?"

Jack climbed back up to the wagon seat, giving his wrists a firm snap. Undaunted, Benjamin began keeping pace.

"Well? What did you do to her?"

"Why do you assume I did something?" He dared a glance at Benjamin, who stared back with a knowing look. Jack sighed loudly, hunching his back. "I accidently called her ugly."

Benjamin threw back his head and roared with laughter.

"How do you accidently call someone ugly? Especially someone that pretty?"

"It's a long story."

"Right," he snickered. "Look, you need to be careful with her. She isn't your wife yet, and that Dewitt character has been eyeing her since he first laid eyes on her."

Jack's jaw tightened as he rested his elbows on his knees, the reins slack in his hands.

107

"Alright," Benjamin said once he gave Jack adequate time to respond. He studied his friend's profile, a feeling of pity coming over him. Jack had sworn off women for himself a long time before, but he was in a hard place. He was practically forced into the marriage, but at the same time, he could have simply said no. Benjamin was sure there was something in his friend that desired a wife and a family. "I'll be towards the back," he finally said and turned his horse.

Jack's head pounded.

How am I going to do this? I don't even know how to talk to her!

Charles Dewitt thundered back to the caravan just before dark, his mare skidding to a stop beside the Baxter's lead wagon.

"Well?" Jack asked, the bite in his voice evident.

"Nothing for at least twenty miles. There's a small town just past the New York line."

"Yeah. Well, Mr. Baxter's fever has broken somewhat, but he still needs a doctor."

"There's one in the next town."

Jack looked at Charles, his eyes narrowed.

"You didn't ride twenty miles in and back in this short time."

"Of course not." Charles's smile was slick and easy. "I met a couple trapper's along the way. I was about to return empty handed so to speak when I found them, and they gave me the information."

"What information?" Piper asked as she came to stand beside Charles's horse.

"There's a town about twenty miles from here. They have a doctor."

Piper frowned. "Twenty miles? That's a long way."

"Jack tells me Mr. Baxter's fever has broken. He'll be better now for the wait."

"I suppose." Piper shifted her weight and grimaced.

Charles's smile faded. "What's wrong with your feet?"

Piper slid her eyes to Jack then back again.

"Oh, it's nothing. I stepped down from the wagon wrong, and twisted my ankle."

Charles dismounted and took one of her hands. No one noticed Jack rolling his eyes.

"May I?" Charles asked.

"It's not proper."

"I assure you it is." He said and dropped to one knee.

Jack looked around quickly. It wasn't the kind of gossip he wanted rolling around the camp: his fiancée holding the hand of

Charles Dewitt as he knelt before her on a bended knee.

Charles dropped her hand and gently picked her hurt foot up and rested it on his knee. He only raised her skirts enough to see the foot and the ankle. He touched and prodded tenderly until Piper hissed. He shot a glare over his shoulder at Jack.

"Well, it's sprained. See that bruising? Swollen a bit too. She's lucky she didn't break it." He set her foot back on the ground and took her hand once again so she could lean some of her weight on him. "A lady needs to be helped from a wagon, Marshall."

"She left the wagon before it was properly stopped."

"Really?" Charles's eyes grew large. "No doubt because you upset her. She doesn't seem like the rash type to me, and jumping from a moving wagon is pretty rash."

"You don't even know her," Jack commented dryly and hopped from the wagon, turning in the same motion to tend to the horses.

"And neither do you, Sir! Imagine the absurdity of bringing a frail woman across the ocean to be your wife!"

Jack spun around, a finger already pointing at Charles's chest. Piper intervened by placing her body between them.

"Stop it! Both of you! I left the wagon of my own accord, and it was not a good decision. It was no one's fault but my own.

Now, stop acting like children!" she said hotly and began limping away. Charles hurried to help her, giving Jack no opportunity to do so himself. He watched them walk away, Charles's voice speaking too lowly for him to interpret what was being said. Bonnie and Mrs. Baxter had their eyes on him and soon pushed their heads together. It was the work of busy mouths for busy bodies. Jack turned back to the horses, a nervous energy eating away at his heart.

Chapter Five

Piper sat straight up, her ears ringing. What had caused the noise? Voices began raising and she slapped her hands over her hears as gunshots rang out around her. Ruth started crying in Bonnie's arms.

"What's happening?" Bonnie cried out and began gathering her children to herself like a mother hen. "Where's my Blaine?"

"I don't know," Piper said quickly. She knew Mr. Brackett had planned to sleep right outside of the wagon. She had been unnerved by the way all of the men had been settling down to sleep on the ground with rifles lying beside them like a child may take a toy to bed. Now she understood why.

Piper dared a peek past the canvas covering at the back of the wagon. A figure darted past, and she thought she recognized the short figure of one of the other wagon owners, Mr. Armstrong, in fast pursuit. The camp erupted in another frenzy of gunfire and voices. Piper clasped both hands over her mouth as what sounded like a body falling could be heard right beside the wagon. She looked at Bonnie and into the wide, fearful eyes of her children. Even the baby had stayed decidedly quiet.

The camp became deathly still, and soon Jack's voice was heard asking for a count of the people to be made. Running footsteps came along the side of the wagon just before the canvas pulled to the side and Jack stuck his head in.

"Are you alright?" he asked Piper, with wide eyes.

She nodded and licked her lips as Jack turned his attention to Bonnie.

"Are you alright, Ma'am?"

"Yes. Is Blaine out there?"

"I haven't seen him yet." Jack gave Piper a final look before ducking back out.

Piper knew it was not good judgment, but she needed to see what had happened. She moved towards the back of the wagon as Bonnie's arm shot forward.

"Piper, no! Don't go out there yet!"

"It's fine. Stay with the children. I'll see if I can find Mr. Brackett."

Bonnie's brown eyes were black in the darkness. "Don't stay out there too long. We don't know if the danger has passed."

"The Lord is my strong tower." Piper tried to smile, and carefully lowered herself to the ground. She tested her hurt ankle and gave herself a moment before limping to the opposite side of the wagon from where people were running to and fro. Piper caught a glimpse of Jack and Benjamin dragging what looked like a man's body between them. She carefully picked her way forward and moved to the back of the Baxter wagon, careful to keep her body hidden and part of her face.

"Is that the last?"

"Yes," Jack confirmed, his face looking down at the body they had just dropped. Piper squinted her eyes and was stunned to see that three other bodies were lying near the one they had just drug over.

"You're hurt?" Benjamin asked.

"It's a flesh wound. A couple of stitches and I'll be fine."

Benjamin shook his head. "I didn't see this coming. We've been too slack."

"Maybe."

"Maybe? Jack, come on. You know we have."

"Something doesn't feel right about this. Did you notice that these men only targeted two wagons?"

"So?"

"So...it was the Armstrong and Baxter wagons. The wagons with the most valuables and money."

Benjamin whistled low. "An inside job."

"Maybe."

Benjamin's head shot upward, and his eyes landed on Piper's peeking form. He nudged Jack and motioned with his head in Piper's direction.

Jack turned and looked down at his hand as Piper's eyes were immediately drawn to the large Colt Walker in his right hand.

"Put that hand cannon back in your holster!" Benjamin hissed. Jack obeyed and went towards Piper holding a hand out.

"You shouldn't be out here," Jack scolded gently.

"I wanted to know what had happened." Even in the scant light, Jack could see how pale she was. Her eyes flicked over to the bodies of the dead men, and her mouth and throat worked like she may be sick.

"Don't let this worry you," Benjamin said, using his body to help block her view. "It's the law of the West and anywhere else for that matter. It's kill or be killed. Jack here knows that all too well." He clasped Jack's shoulder and gave it a shake. "That's why he carries that hand cannon," he laughed.

Jack offered a nervous laugh himself, but let it die in his chest as he looked back at Piper. She was looking at them like they were monsters.

"Sweetheart," Benjamin began. "Respect is like a weapon all by itself out here. Sometimes you can calm a situation by using or demanding respect, but you always go armed with a real weapon too. Sometimes there is time for talk, but the rest of the time…is for bullets." He touched her shoulder kindly. "Why don't you help Jack get cleaned up? I'm sure he could use your help. I'll get another couple of hands and take care of things out here."

Jack nodded and moved towards Piper, taking her by her hands. He gently led her away, careful to not move too quickly because of her foot and ankle.

"I have some supplies in my saddle bag."

"Thank God! There you are!" a familiar voice cried out, silhouetted against a freshly stoked fire. Charles ran up to the pair and unabashedly took Piper's hands from Jack's.

"I'm all right, Charles." She responded with a tight-lipped smile. "I can't say the same for a few others, including Jack. Please excuse us. Jack's been hurt."

"Oh…I'm…sorry to hear that Marshall."

Jack regarded Charles with a growing sense of dislike. His words didn't match the glint in his eyes whatsoever. Jack began to wonder if Charles would like nothing better than to see him removed from Piper permanently.

"Charles, Marshall Graves has an unpleasant task ahead of him tonight. Perhaps you could see about helping him?"

Charles nodded soberly. "Sure, Piper. I can do that."

"Thank you." She smiled tightly again and moved away from him with Jack.

"I'm sure he wishes I had just died," Jack grumbled.

"Now why would he wish such a horrible thing?" Piper's voice held a tremor that hadn't been present earlier. He hoped the reality had hit her that he could have died and that she might be sorry. He suspected it had more to do with seeing the bodies.

"I think the reason is obvious." He couldn't see her face properly, but he was sure she was blushing.

"I'm going to let Bonnie know I'm alright. Sit by the fire, and I'll be right back."

Jack got his supplies and took a seat on the ground next to the fire. The excitement of the evening was already washing away, and he was left with the guilt of having shot two men. How could he explain to Piper that this was just the way it was? Benjamin had told it just fine, but he had left out the human aspect of it. He had to shoot those men, but he still felt guilty. They had lost one of their own from the caravan, and that number was one too many, but would it have been higher if he hadn't done what he had.

"Bonnie wishes you well, and sent a couple extra pieces of cloth in case you need them." Piper eased herself down beside him and watched with catching breath as Jack removed his vest and then his shirt. The shirt had a tear along the left arm and was soaked in blood.

"Was it a gunshot or a knife?" Her lips puckered in a frown as she inspected the wound.

"A knife," Jack winced as he poured water from his canteen over the wound. "There's some fine thread and a needle right here beside me. Run some water over that needle and then hand it to me, please."

Piper did as she was told. She had seen the local doctor stitch her father's leg after a nasty fall down the front steps once before, but it was a far more sterile affair; not something done by a campfire in the wee hours of the morning while bandits were being placed in shallow graves nearby.

She watched in silence as Jack threaded the needle and asked her to pour more water over the wound. He had several old scars on his arm and one deep and wide scar just under his collar bone. She was curious about the scars she could see and the ones she was sure existed out of her sight, but what caught her attention more was the way Jack's muscle looked in the firelight. He wasn't a bulky man. He was formed from tight, sinewy muscle. The normally covered flesh of his back and chest was a shade or two lighter than the skin of his face, neck, and hands. It proved he was a man who didn't shy away from the outdoors and from the work he had to do. She wondered what that tight muscle would feel like under her fingertips. She wondered if his skin would smell of the earth he was so accustomed to roaming.

"Piper?"

Piper blinked and ran her tongue over her lips.

"I'm sorry. Did you say something?"

Jack suppressed the laugh that tried to skip past his lips. He had seen how she had been looking at him.

"I asked if you would get me a clean shirt from my saddle bags."

"Oh. Yes. Of course." Piper pushed herself up from the ground and went to Jack's horse. She returned as promptly as she could under the circumstances of her injury with a neatly folded shirt of some dark color. He seemed to only wear dark colors.

"I'm sorry you had to see the bodies, Piper."

Piper didn't want a reminder of what she had seen. She doubted she would ever forget it.

"You did what you felt you needed to, Jack. I don't have to like it or approve of it."

Jack looked at her while he chose his words carefully.

129

"Piper, you realize I will still be a Marshall after we are married. I don't plan on bringing my work home with me, but you will have to come to terms with the fact that sometimes I have to do ugly things to keep others safe."

Piper touched her skirts, her head angled downward. Jack couldn't read her expression, and it unnerved him.

"I understand, Jack. I just..."

"You just what?"

"I just don't know if I can live with it." She raised her head, and he could see a defiant positioning of her features. Her face might as well have been a brick wall.

"So...you're saying that you may not marry me?"

"I don't know what I'm saying yet. I need some time to think."

Jack nodded and twisted his mouth to one side, moving his eyes to the fire.

"You do that, Piper. In the meantime, I'll just keep doing my job, protecting the people of this caravan."

Later, as the sun began to streak the sky with pink, Piper fell into a fitful sleep. Jack's words haunted her and made her feel guilty. But the thing that interrupted her sleep the most was the mental images of Jack's bare chest in the firelight.

Chapter Six

"You should ride with me today," Charles insisted, as he smiled at Piper.

"I can't ride a horse, Charles."

"No, but you can ride in my carriage."

Piper looked up at him quickly.

"The little carriage is yours?"

"Yes, although it will need new wheels I'm afraid by the time we reach Detroit. I just couldn't leave it behind. It's too attractive."

Piper smiled. "I thought it was a fine looking carriage when I first saw it! I love the fringe around the roof. Why haven't you been using it?"

"Well now, I couldn't ride my horse and drive the buggy. I hired William over there to drive it for me. It's been a long time since I could just be in the saddle enjoying the outdoors."

William gave Piper a wave, and her smile disappeared. If there was a person in the caravan who frightened Piper, it was William. He was young as it were, but he had a weathered angry look about him, that made him appear older. He was generally un-kept most of the time.

"Had he worked for you in Boston?"

"Sometimes. I felt bad for him and offered for him to do this. He might have a better shot in Detroit." He smiled down at her. "You know, a fresh start."

"That's kind of you. You must be a humanitarian at heart."

"I try my best."

"Let me tell Bonnie. I'll be right back."

Charles called after her, his gaze following her from under his lashes.

"Better tell Jack too."

Piper's footsteps halted their uneven gait. She glanced back once.

"No need for that." She turned back and began limping again.

Charles looked back at William, and they smiled at each other in a matching conniving way.

Jack poked around the field for several minutes trying to find the best wildflowers he could. He preferred the flowers of fall and their darker colors, but the pastels of spring were nice too. He wanted to find a few of the prettiest. Piper deserved the prettiest. He had missed having her in the wagon seat beside him, and when Benjamin had ridden up to inform him that she was riding in the little buggy with Charles, he knew he had better start doing something to win her heart. He didn't want her to go to back to England. He certainly didn't want to live in Detroit with her if she was intent on someone else. He wouldn't want to risk running into her and say Charles Dewitt on the street. She was here now. She was here to be his wife. He wanted her to be his wife. She was head strong and a bit of a snob, but there was something about Piper Renwick that had stirred something within him. He didn't want to have to choose another.

He wrapped a broken stem around his gathered flowers and studied the bouquet with a critical eye.

"Well, now, that's right pretty."

Jack grunted and refused to look at Benjamin. He was losing his touch. He hadn't even realized his friend had approached.

"You better get a move on with your courtship. Piper and Charles have been giggling and having a good ole time over there on that blanket eating their lunch. Bets around the camp are that she will be a Dewitt once we reach Detroit and not a Walker."

Jack lifted his head to see if Benjamin had his joking face on. He sighed audibly once he saw that he didn't.

"I can't just waltz over there and give her these with Charles Dewitt sitting there."

"Sure you can. She's spoken for. Spoken for by you." Benjamin poked him in the arm.

"Ow! Easy on my arm!"

"You need something to rile you up. Now get over there! Look he's packing things up anyway."

Jack watched as Charles began carrying what was left of their lunch back to the buggy. He hurried over as Piper began folding the blanket they had been sitting on.

"Piper?"

Piper turned slowly and glanced down at the small bouquet he held out to her.

"What's this?"

"I…uh…picked these for you."

She didn't take the bouquet and shook her head instead.

"Are these little wildflowers supposed to make things right between us?"

"I want them to be a start."

"You'll have to do better than that," she replied coldly. "Tell me. The advertisement your father placed; did you prompt him on what to say? Perhaps you pulled your big gun out and held it to his head?"

"What are you talking about?"

"I was expecting a gentleman, Jack! An educated, intelligent gentleman! What I got was a rough man who kills for a living! The advertisement was a lie!"

A hush fell over the camp as Piper, with red cheeks, let out her pent up disappointments and anger.

"Nothing in that advertisement was a lie. The only thing omitted was that I'm a Marshall. I don't know why he didn't put that in. I wasn't present for the creation of that advertisement." Jack allowed the hand that held the bouquet to fall beside his thigh. He couldn't keep the hurt from his eyes or his voice. Piper was undaunted by either.

"Perhaps you should have taken your marital affairs into your own hand instead of relying on your father."

"You were in the same fix as me. We were both commanded to marry. Both of our fathers had a hand in this."

"It's different for women, and you know it, Jack."

"I don't rightly know anything, Piper." Jack cast a defeated look over Piper's shoulder at Charles's smug face before turning away. He stopped where a little girl of about ten was playing with her doll on the grass.

"Here you go, sweetie," he said and handed her the flowers.

"These are pretty. Thank you," she said and shyly took them from his hand.

"I'm glad you think so," Jack said and walked away as proudly as he could through all the watching eyes.

Piper sat upright, her body rigid and her heart hammering. There had been gunshots again. Again! She scrambled to the back of the wagon, a bizarre repeat of the night before happening again, right down to Bonnie sitting up and gathering her children to her hen style.

"Oh Lord, not again!" she cried out.

"Stay here!" Piper worked her way from the back of the wagon ignoring Bonnie's cautions and begging for her to stay.

The chaos was twofold compared to the night before. She could hear a woman's scream, and closed her eyes momentarily, her hand bracing herself against the wagon.

Father, please protect us!

Piper eased around the edge of the wagon just enough so she could see the center area where the campfires from the evening before had been burning. Men were running, guns drawn, the light of the full moon reflecting off of the dark metal. She caught a glimpse of Jack as he ducked behind a tree, his voice ringing out sharp orders for

Benjamin. She wondered momentarily who was the higher ranking Marshall.

Piper moved backward, her breath catching in her throat as a pair of rough hands grabbed her. She screamed, flinging her arms overhead as she tried to land blows on whoever her assailant was. Rough fabric was pulled over her head, and she could smell a musty odor as if the fabric had held old potatoes.

"Shut up!" the voice commanded. "Shut up, or I'll break your pretty little neck!"

Piper struggled as her body was lifted from the ground, but she clamped her mouth shut as she was instructed. She cursed the wide skirt and petticoat over the flexible caging beneath. Women didn't stand a fair chance in a situation like this with all the many layers of clothing they had to wear.

Another set of hands was on her, and she felt her body being lifted higher. Soon air blew around and under the sack over her head as the horse she was sitting sideways on took off at a gallop. The man controlling the animal called out as he left the campsite: "I have her!"

Several guns fired, and Piper felt the man bend over her, his lips uttering more curses than she had ever heard at once. She was positive she heard the hiss and whizz of a bullet coming close to her face. She fought tears as the sounds of the camp became distant, and the horse's hooves pounding the earth became more distinct. More horses soon joined, but she couldn't distinguish how many. Riotous laughter echoed around her; a celebration for their sin.

Lord Jesus, please deliver me from their hands.

"Jack!" Benjamin turned a full circle in the middle of the camp, his eyes wide and desperately searching. "Jack!"

"Here!" Jack called, his head bowed over Mr. Baxter. Mrs. Baxter let out a wail as Jack looked up at her and shook his head. He staggered to his feet, his mind filled with rage as he watched the older woman lay her body over her husband's.

"He was trying to protect the money," Jack said as Benjamin stood by his side.

"Jack..." Benjamin began. His voice was strange, and Jack looked him full in the face.

"What?"

"They took Charles Dewitt. And..."

"And what?" Jack yelled, grabbing his friend by the shoulders.

"And Piper."

Jack let go of Benjamin and backed away, his head spinning and his stomach forcing bile up his throat.

"Eight," Jack said. "There was eight of them. That means that originally there was eleven."

Benjamin nodded. He knew Jack needed to allow his Marshall instincts to take over. He needed to hunt. His emotions would have to wait.

"We'll get them." Benjamin nodded.

Jack holstered his gun.

"We'll get them, and then they will die."

Benjamin watched the determined back of Jack as he began taking an assessment of the damages and helping the injured. He had no doubt that was exactly what Jack planned on doing once they caught up with them.

Chapter Seven

What was left of the caravan began moving forward before the sun had risen. The sky had the lighter navy blue color of predawn, but Jack couldn't wait. The gang hadn't taken all the money, there was more in another wagon, and they couldn't take any chances. Plus, there was the injured who needed tending. Mr. Baxter was dead, several others were shot or stabbed and may not live, and Piper and Charles had been kidnapped. Plus, another man was missing, William the hired buggy driver of Dewitt's. No one had seen him since the attack, and Jack couldn't waste valuable time looking. Maybe he had been taken hostage too.

Jack looked up at the boy of no more than fourteen whom he had asked to drive the Baxter wagon. He looked down at Jack, his face pale, and his eyes unsure.

"You'll do fine. Another wagon will go ahead of you, just follow. Have you never driven a wagon before?"

He shook his light colored head. "No, Sir...I mean yes, just not one this size, and not over rough ground."

Jack smiled reassuringly. "You'll be fine. You're going to do your father proud. Your brother is driving the family wagon and you're driving this one. Your Dad would be bursting with pride for the two of you."

The boy nodded and seemed to relax. Jack wished someone could give him a pep talk. He mounted his horse and waited for Benjamin to give the word that the rear was ready.

Piper. Piper, I will find you, and then I will give you whatever you want. If you want freedom, you can have it. If you want a fancy house void of a farm, you can have it. By God, if you want Charles Dewitt, you can have him! I'll marry you off myself; just please, please be alright.

"Rear is ready. I have two men with rifles back there. You and I will lead, with an occasional ride to the back to check on things." Benjamin gave Jack a critical eye when he saw the distant look on his face.

"We'll get them, Jack, but first we need to get to that town to make a plan and to see about our injured."

"I know." Jack moved to the lead wagon, the Brackett wagon of all things, and gave Blaine Brackett a nod. "We're ready."

Blaine responded with a nod of his own, and slapped the reins over the horse's backs, as Benjamin and Jack took their spots at the lead.

"You know it was the Faceless Gang, right?" Benjamin asked from the corner of his mouth once sufficient distance was put between them and the Brackett wagon. There was no need for more hysteria.

"I saw the bandanas and pillow cases with the eye holes poked through."

Benjamin worked his mouth. Jack was a dangerous man on a good day, and that particular day wasn't good, making him even more lethal.

"Spit it out, Ben."

"This isn't their norm. You know, hitting a smaller caravan back to back. They stick mainly to trains…and much larger caravans…but mainly trains."

"You thinking inside job?"

"Yeah, I am."

Jack sighed. "I was too. I was also thinking that the two men who are missing are Charles Dewitt and his hired hand." He slid his eyes to Benjamin. "Don't you find that odd?"

"I do, but I saw Charles get tackled and thrown on a horse. Bonnie saw Piper being drug away." He shrugged. "Looks like William is it."

"Not necessarily," Jack countered, his voice low.

"Why?"

"What better farce than to pretend to be kidnapped? It would open up a whole world of possibilities. Night before? Yeah, that was a dry run to see what would happen. To see what we would do." Jack shook his head, his eyes narrowed. "Two Marshalls only for a caravan that's transporting mainly businessmen and their families and bankers and theirs, with a ton of gold and silver, not to mention the paper money. It was bad from the beginning. Should have had at least four Marshalls."

"What's done is done, Jack."

"That part is done. Their part is coming."

"You know as..."

"Leave it alone." Jack warned. Benjamin stared at him for a moment knowing that the time wasn't right for him to hear what needed to be said. It would have to wait.

"That lying piece of..." Benjamin's words were cut off by Jack racing back. His face said it all.

"Dewitt lied. The town is only another three miles. It wasn't twenty! It was no more than ten! If that!"

"I don't understand why he would have lied."

Jack looked at Benjamin pointedly.

"Ah. Yes." Benjamin nodded. "Wasn't really looking for a town. He was meeting up with the hiding gang."

"You're a truly smart one," Jack said dryly. "Get everyone moving again. We can't afford a break. I want to be in that town before nightfall."

"You planning on us going after them after dark?" Benjamin asked, a warning tone in his voice.

"Won't be the first time we've done something like it."

"Yeah, but that was one or two people…not eight…or more."

Jack's dark look closed Benjamin's mouth. He turned his horse to take care of the task himself.

"Lord, I do believe Black Hands has fallen in love."

The town stretched out before them, many buildings and movement promising the help they would need. The rain that had threatened for two days had finally come, but it was only a light drizzle, and Jack wasn't worried it would hinder his pursuit. If anything the damp ground would yield crisper footprints and other telltale signs that he would need.

"Get the injured ones to the town doctor first," Jack told Blaine Brackett.

"What are you going to do?"

"Benjamin and I are going to speak to the town Sheriff."

"Good thinking." Blaine nodded. I'll get the sick ones settled and then see about room accommodations." He shook his head. "Piper will be sorely missed for the bartering."

Benjamin shot Jack a quick look as Piper's name flew carelessly from Blaine's lips. He saw the jaw muscle pop his beard out, but he said nothing.

"Let's go, Jack."

Jack and Benjamin trotted their horses down the hillside out of the main tree line that seemed to encase the town in a horseshoe shape. The Sheriff's office wasn't hard to find. It was the center building on the main street, and the upstairs had heavy iron bars over the windows. Jack looked upward and could see hands dangling through the bars. It was obvious they already had a few visitors. His heart leaped with a dangerous hope that the cells held the Faceless Gang and Piper was somewhere in the town safe and unharmed. His skin crawled whenever his mind jumped ahead of itself, and he imagined the horrors that might be happening to her.

They dismounted and loosely tied their horse reins to the fence posting above the complimentary watering trough. Benjamin followed Jack onto the wooden walkway and into the Sheriff's office. A man of about forty looked up from papers on his desk, his salt and pepper hair slightly ruffled. Gray eyes flicked towards their gun holsters.

"Can I help you, boys?"

Jack moved the lapel of his jacket to reveal the star he wore. "I'm U.S. Marshall Jack Walker, and this is Marshall Benjamin Graves."

The Sheriff leaned back in his chair and regarded Jack with an amused expression.

"Are you Black Hands Walker?" He looked pointedly at the black leather gloves sitting snuggly on Jack's hands.

"I am."

159

He tossed his head back and laughed. Jack and Benjamin exchanged an uneasy look. The Sheriff stood and extended a hand over the desk.

"You're a legend, son."

Jack shook his hand. "I am?"

"You bet you are. Hey, Will, come in here and meet a real life legend!" The Sheriff held a hand to Benjamin as well, as a young man entered from another room. His red hair and freckles reminded Jack of the Brackett boys.

"I'm Sheriff Poole, and this is my deputy Will Rodgers."

Jack felt the air deflate from his lungs.

"You only have one deputy?"

"For right now I do."

Jack shook his head and looked at Benjamin.

"This isn't going to work."

Sheriff Poole looked from one man to the other.

"What's not going to work?"

Benjamin quickly explained how the caravan had left Boston headed for Detroit and what the caravan purpose was. He gave a condensed version of the two attacks, with the final bit of information spoken softly.

"They also took Jack's fiancée."

"Oh." The Sheriff shook his head. "I've heard of that gang of outlaws, but I didn't think they would be much of a problem here.

161

They were mainly hitting trains and stagecoaches on the East Coast, right?"

"Yes, we think so, but they may be responsible for a few robberies as far west as Ohio."

"They work fast. This isn't easy terrain to go over. I mean the closer you are to the coast it is, but not here in upper state. Our biggest problems are the occasional runaway slave or Indian that's left behind causing trouble."

"Did a band of men come through here last night?" Jack asked through clenched teeth. He had no interest in the problems of that little town.

"Nope. Not that we know of. We would have noticed a group of that size riding together. Especially if they had only a single woman with them."

"Do you have a map?"

"Sure." Sheriff Poole nodded and whispered to Deputy Rodgers. The young man hurried from the room, returning swiftly with two large rolled documents. The Sheriff took one and moved things on his desk so he could spread it out.

"Now, it's not a great one, but it does show a forty mile radius of the town." He pointed a rough finger on the western edge of the map. "Just imagine past this area. That's going to be Albany. It's a far larger place than here."

"Yes, I've been there," Jack commented. "I was purposefully not hitting

163

all of the bigger places on our trip. Sometimes a city can pose more danger for a caravan than the wilderness."

"I understand that."

Jack studied the map with his weight held on the palms of his hands. The others watched in silence as he pointed to a spot east of the town.

"Is the terrain still accurate?"

"Ohm, pretty much. I had this made about fifteen months ago."

Jack spoke softly. "This was about where we were last night." He lifted his eyes to Benjamin's. "See the clearing and the varied tree copses?"

"I see."

"Do you have a pencil?"

"I do." The Sheriff picked one up from the edge of the desk and handed it to Jack.

Jack licked the lead tip and lightly marked the spot he had indicated, before tracing a line in two directions away from the spot.

"If they wanted to avoid towns or largely populated areas they would have taken these routes. See how they can go around this town from either way to get to Albany?"

"Do you think that's where they would go?" Benjamin asked.

"I think that's where they would go for the time being. It's easier to get lost in a place that size than one like here." Jack straightened. I think the north route is more likely. Too many farms and little hamlets along the south."

Benjamin studied the map. "I see what you're saying." He pointed to a pale blue line running parallel to the route Jack had traced. "Are these streams?"

"They're rivers. The one going north that intersects the one going west is the Hudson, and the other that continues on past Albany is the Mohawk."

"They'll stay near the rivers," Jack said with certainty. He looked at Marshall Poole. "Do you have available men that you use for militia reasons?"

The Sheriff stared at him blankly.

"I mean…I have two honorary deputies for different things."

"I don't have time to wait for more Marshalls I need a couple more people to assist in this."

"Right. Let me see what I can do. Give me until morning."

"I'll give you until nightfall."

The Sheriff nodded slowly. "Alright, Marshall Walker. I'll do what I can."

Jack and Benjamin left the Sheriff's office with directions to the doctor. They checked on the two men with gunshot wounds, both serious enough that they would be spending the evening in the infirmary. The few others with minor injuries were already treated. Jack was grateful that the two serious injuries were men who were traveling alone. There had been enough heartache and trauma for the women. He noticed Mrs. Baxter staring with a faraway look on her face into the front door of the doctor's building. She wrung her hands unconsciously, her face still blotted and red.

"Mrs. Baxter?" Jack asked gently. "Is there something I can do for you?"

"He was a fool," she whispered.

"Excuse me?"

She turned watery eyes up to Jack's face. "My husband was a fool. Why would he think at our age that we should go tromping through the wilderness to a new city? Boston had been good to us. We had weathered the trials of starting a new bank there. We had even survived my closed womb." A skinny tear fell past her gray lashes. "He was a fool."

Jack didn't know what to say. How could he comfort her? He opened his mouth and hoped that his words wouldn't be crass or too short.

"I'm sure he thought he was doing a good thing." Jack placed an arm around her shoulder and began leading her away. Mr. Baxter was buried at the scene of his death. There was nothing for her in the doctor's office. "He died bravely, Mrs. Baxter. He died protecting the money." Jack shook his head, knowing that wasn't entirely true. "He died protecting you."

A brittle sob escaped her lips, and she laid her head against Jack's chest as he continued to lead her. He was looking for one person in particular, and once he found her and their eyes met, she came immediately.

Bonnie shifted baby Ruth to her opposite hip and replaced Jack's arm around Mrs. Baxter's shoulder. Jack dug out three dollars from his pocket and several pieces of silver.

"Make sure she is tended to tonight. Don't let her be alone for too long," he said quietly. "I'll replace whatever money you and Blaine have to put out."

"I won't let her alone, Marshall. You just see to getting Miss Piper back."

"I will." Jack watched the heavier younger woman lead the frail older one away.

He knew Bonnie had enough on her with her own children, but he couldn't think of a better person to look after the grieving widow. Bonnie had a big heart; it was obvious even to him.

"Jack, we need to talk." Benjamin came to his side once the women were out of earshot.

"Alright, Ben. Let's get a drink. I sorely need one."

"No, you don't."

Jack followed his friend to the nearest hotel, surprised to find that the town had two separate ones. He had no doubt that the one at the southern end of the street was more of a brothel, and made a mental note to tell

Bonnie and the other women to keep their men clear of that one.

Benjamin pointed to a table and then went to the bar, returning with two small mugs of coffee.

"Coffee?"

"Yes. We both need to be clear headed right now."

"What do you want to talk about? Besides the fact that you don't think we should begin the search tonight?"

"I've come to grips with that. We need to get a move on. Time's wasting."

"I'm glad you see my point of view."

Benjamin toyed with the mug and looked at Jack hard.

"I need to know that your head is right."

"My head is always right."

"No, it isn't. Not this time."

Jack sighed. "What can I say, Ben? They took Piper."

"You love her?"

Jack looked up expecting to see the usual teasing expression or jovial look that Benjamin seemed to sport at all times, but at that moment his face was stone serious.

"I do love her. I can't say why, seeing as how I can't even talk to her. I think I might have loved her since I first saw her red hair peeking out from under her bonnet as she struggled to drag her trunk, by herself, down the ship's gangplank."

"That's why your head isn't on straight. This gang is dangerous. They're a loose cannon in the way they tested us before actually taking what they wanted." He rubbed at the several days' worth of stubble on his chin and cheeks. "You can't go off half-cocked with Piper being the only thing on your mind. There's people's fortunes at stake, and there's justice to think about. You can't just kill all of them, Jack."

"I know that."

"You said you were going to kill them all."

Jack leaned over the table, his brown eyes hard like flint.

"I will kill whomever I need to if it means getting her and the money back." He leaned back against the chair again, his eyes steady. "Is that better?"

"Vengeance is mine, sayeth the Lord."

"Don't start with that. You live like a heathen half the time, yet when you want to drive a point home, you bring out Holy Scripture. It isn't right."

"I know it, but you better wrap your mind around it. Your little woman is a Christian." He lifted his hands palms outward before bringing his fingers down in dismissal. "We both should pay better attention. How many times do you think God spared our lives?"

"More than a few," Jack agreed, sipping at the hot black coffee.

"Exactly. Maybe once we're done with this, we should look into real salvation, my friend." Benjamin eyed him warily expecting protest, laughter, or downright anger; but all he received was Jack staring moodily into his coffee mug.

"Maybe you're right." Jack lifted his eyes, and Benjamin despised the sadness he saw there. "I didn't try hard enough with her. I shouldn't have tried to work with her coming at the same time. I did little to make her time easier. I mean the blanket separating the room the day she arrived seemed to please her, and me asking her to ride with me after Baxter took sick, but I made that flower bouquet too late."

"Jack," Benjamin shook his head. "She's in an entirely new country, away from her loved ones, and let's face it; you can be rough, but she didn't run away screaming the first day. She has heart, and I do believe she's tough as nails. So, Charles Dewitt stole her attention? If he's what we think he is, she won't have eyes for anyone but you once this thing is over."

Chapter Eight

Piper was weary of the sway of the wagon. She was weary of Charles's hot back rubbing against hers. But mostly, she was weary of the bandana that was forced between her teeth and the sack still over her head. The itchy material had left a rash along her cheeks, and she could feel it burning and itching.

The wagon finally stopped, and Piper breathed in the fresh night air as she was untied from Charles and helped from the back of the wagon. The hands handling her that evening were far gentler than the one's from the night before. She could smell burning firewood and hear snickers and coarse talk as her sack and bandana were removed. William was the first face she focused on. As soon as the bandana was untied, she allowed her tongue to begin its lashing.

"You traitorous man! Mr. Dewitt hired you out of the goodness of his heart to drive his buggy, and you…you…spat in his face!"

William laughed, exposing his missing teeth.

"You think so? How 'bout you ask him about his buggy."

Charles stepped in front of Piper, rubbing at his wrists where they had been tied for almost a full day. He smiled sheepishly at her.

"Wasn't my buggy, darling. I stole that in Boston before we left. The morning we left to be exact. I needed a viable excuse for William to be with me."

"What?" Piper looked from Charles to William and then at the eight faces lit by the crackling fire. "I don't understand."

"It was my plan. I had to be part of the caravan to understand how to handle the Marshalls. You...well you were a pleasant surprise."

"You planned that attack?" she yelled, her eyes bulging from the sockets.

"Yes, both of them." Charles smiled. It made Piper's skin crawl to see how proud that smile was. "The ride out to see about a town and a doctor? Yes, that was a ruse so I could meet with my gang, who had followed stealthily, I might add. Good job boys, really." Charles clapped lightly as a few men gave elaborate mock bows. "Benjamin and Jack were not enough. I was quite pleased to know that only two Marshalls would be in attendance. I was a little worried about your fiancée, though." Charles waggled a finger, arching one eyebrow. "Black Hands Walker is known from Texas to Boston, and his reputation precedes him. He's one of the toughest lawmen to ever walk the earth."

Piper swallowed against the constriction on her throat. Her eyes stung. Jack. How could she have been so blinded?

Because you turned your eyes away from God and coveted what he hadn't portioned for you.

A tear slipped from each corner of her eyes. Charles wiped at them with a thumb, his face sympathetic.

"Now don't cry, Piper. You will see in time that this was for the best. I can afford to give you a life you deserve. A life that Jack Walker could only dream of giving you." He moved her by the shoulders and helped her onto a log that had been placed near the fire. "Now, I'm going to untie you, but don't make me regret it."

Piper breathed out audibly as she was finally allowed to bring her aching arms to the front. Her shoulder joints felt like they had been pulled and twisted out of socket.

"What did you boys find for use to eat?"

"Three rabbits, and we took all of the food supplies from that front wagon."

Piper felt a pang of anger. She knew they were speaking of the Baxter wagon. What had Mrs. Baxter given Mr. Baxter to eat? He was just getting some strength back. She wanted to refuse food from the criminals, but as she watched the rabbits get skinned and soon smelled the heady aroma of fresh meat cooking, her stomach responded with a loud grumble and cramp of protest for how empty it was. She could practically feel her saliva glands engaging.

Once dinner was finished cooking, Charles fixed her a plate and brought it to her. There was a meager amount of rabbit and rough bread.

"I will wine and dine you like a Queen once we reach Albany."

Piper ate the sinewy greasy, yet delicious meat, running her bread over the tin plate to gather the leftover grease onto the bread. She sighed dejectedly that there wasn't more.

"I don't want to be wined and dined, Mr. Dewitt."

"Aw, now don't go back to calling me that! We're on a first name basis!"

"Not anymore we aren't," Piper replied hotly. "I was a fool for falling for your smooth talk and gentleman's ways. You were a wolf in sheep's clothing."

"You'll see the great benefits you will reap once this is behind us. Just think of the things we can have. The home we can build together!"

Piper shook her head. "I want nothing with you or from you, Charles."

His face fell slowly, and she watched a dangerous look enter his green eyes. It reflected in the firelight, and the brilliant color was like something tainted with black poison.

"You'll change your mind, or perhaps you will be of no more use to me. Perhaps you would be of better use to some of the men of this camp."

185

Piper swallowed as his words sunk in. She dared a glance around the campfire and saw greedy grins from all sides. One man rose and tilted her head up roughly by the chin. He smelled horrible, and the skin of his hand was like bark. She jerked her head away, her eyes filling with tears. She heard a faint click as the men went silent. Charles had a pistol pointed at the back of the man's head.

"I didn't say she was available now. Until I say, she's off limits. Understand?"

"Sure, Dewitt," the man said and raised his hands slowly. "I'll just go back to my supper now."

"Yes, you do that." Charles sat back down beside Piper but kept his gun beside him.

Oh Lord Jesus, please forgive me for my pride. My pride has put me in this predicament. Your word says you are my strength and shield. Please, honor that and send help! Please send the man I should have honored to begin with. Please send Jack!

Piper laid in the wagon and cried silently. How could she withstand the course language and ogling from the men? How could she keep herself from having to go into danger at the next robbery? And another robbery was inevitable. Men like the ones she was forced to be with had insatiable appetites for what didn't belong to them.

The canvas at the back of the wagon pulled to the side, and Piper sat up as Charles hopped easily into the back of the wagon.

"What do you want?"

"I wanted to speak with you." He sat close to her, and she could smell whiskey on his breath.

"I'm trying to sleep."

"Let's sleep together then," he chuckled and nuzzled his face against her neck.

Piper pushed at his shoulders angrily.

"Stop that!"

"Why, Kitten? I know you feel the same way about me. You're just mad right now."

"Right now? Not just right now! Forever!"

Charles laughed and pressed his lips hard against her mouth, pulling her by her upper arms so that she was laying on top of him.

"No!" Piper yelled and managed to get her knee up and forward, striking him firmly in the groin.

Charles's eyes bulged in the darkness, and his mouth made a perfect O as he reached for his injured area. A hiss and strangled cry escaped his open mouth. Piper felt a satisfying moment of triumph. It didn't matter what kind of punishment he would inflict.

"William!" Charles finally managed to call, the single word strangled causing him to repeat it. The opening to the back of the wagon opened again, and William peeked inside. His surprised expression swiftly turned to one of amusement.

Charles pulled himself to the back of the wagon.

"Tie her back up!"

"Sure, boss."

Charles watched Piper warily until William returned, embarrassedly holding his hand out so William could help him from the wagon. Piper smiled as she heard loud laughter and ridiculous statements being hurled at Charles as he emerged from the wagon and staggered away.

"No trouble out of you, girl," William said with a growl.

"I have no intentions unless you want to try something foolish too." She looked up at him, her blue eyes defiant.

"No Ma'am."

Piper sighed as the fading satisfaction gave way to the returning worry. William finished tying her hands and ankles and laid her down on her side, before leaving without another word. Soon the camp was quiet, and the glow of the campfire died.

"Jack," she whispered to the darkness. "Please don't be so angry that you won't come for me."

Chapter Nine

The wagon began moving just before the sky opened to the sunlight. Piper couldn't see it yet, but the wagon was gathering a dim grayish light, and she knew that soon the sky would fill with pink and yellow.

No one had come to allow her a chance to relieve herself, or to even bring her so much as a sip of water from a canteen. The day was going to be hot. Her hair was already sticking to the back of her neck.

Piper turned her body and began raising both legs at once to kick at the side of the wagon.

"Hello?" She kicked again. "Hello?"

The wagon slowly rolled to a stop, and soon the angry face of Charles Dewitt was centered at the back of the wagon, the canvas flap held firmly in one hand.

"What, Piper? What do you need?"

"I need to relieve myself, and I would like some water."

His face morphed into a sneer.

"After what you pulled last night you think I should accommodate you?"

"I think you better do something, Charles, or I will just scream bloody murder. Maybe we will see how close the Marshalls really are, or perhaps it will be a test to see if the Indians are really gone from this area. I hear the Iroquois are quite hospitable."

Charles chewed on his lip debating whether to call her bluff. Piper opened her mouth and sucked in air, but he quickly brought his hands up and hopped into the wagon to untie her.

"You're a hard woman to deal with," he grumbled as he fumbled with the rope.

"Thank you," Piper said and rubbed at her wrists as he began working on the rope at her ankles.

"You thank me for that statement?"

"I thank you for untying me."

"Don't try anything stupid. I'll be close, and I'll have a man on you with a rifle before you can blink your pretty little eyes."

"I have no intention of running. It would serve no purpose."

"I do admire your intelligence," he responded and helped her from the wagon.

The morning moved on at a slow pace. Piper could feel sweat dripping from her temples and down the back of her neck as the wagon finally rolled to a stop. She listened, her head angled to the side.

Water. We're near water.

She could have cried from relief. If she played her cards right, Charles might allow her to wade into whatever body of water it was and scrub at her hands and face. For not the first time since coming to America, she cursed the layers of fabric she as a woman was expected to wear. America or England, it didn't matter, but the weight of it was exhausting.

The canvas pulled back, and Piper blinked against the sunlight.

"Come on, Piper. We need to cross the river. You'll have to go on foot or horseback now."

"I hardly think…"

William scowled at her, causing deep lines to form on his face.

"We don't rightly care what you think! Now get a move on it!"

Piper gave him a sharp look.

"Untie me and I shall."

William huffed but entered the wagon and untied her ankles, leading her out roughly by her tied hands.

Piper looked at the river in front of her. It was wide, and she had a hard time seeing the other side. Had it been a different circumstance, she would have taken the time to admire the beauty which surrounded it. The bank edged its way slowly to the water's edge, and there was a little area that was clear of the trees that demanded space right up to the water's edge. She looked across and could see rock sharing space with trees on the other side. Water rushed past, and she followed the progression with her eyes.

She could see the top of a wide waterfall not far off.

"If we try to cross here the current will pull us over that fall."

Charles came forward and relieved William of his Piper duties. He cut her ropes with a sharp knife. His eyes dark as he looked down on her.

"I have cut your ties. Cross me again and I'll either hand you to the men or use this to slit your pretty throat. Do you understand?" He moved the knife back and forth in front of her face, sunlight catching the blade.

Piper stared up at him, her face unreadable.

"You surely know how to court a lady."

"You had your shot at that. Once we get to Albany, we may be able to start anew."

Piper rubbed at her wrists as Charles spoke quickly to the men waiting for their orders. She exhaled slowly as she heard him heed her warning. They would move further up river before attempting to cross.

"We should cross over where the Mohawk meets," William suggested. "We have to cross it to get to Albany anyway unless you want to go further north."

"No," Charles confirmed. "I do not. Further north will almost guarantee a run in with the Iroquois. Besides, further north will leave us vulnerable. The Marshalls have no doubt regrouped with help by now."

Jack moved over the rock on his belly, his eyes tracking the group. When he first caught sight of Piper, he had fought the urge to just run down the rock and grab her from their clutches, but it wasn't wise, and he knew it.

"They're going to cross," Benjamin breathed at his side. He turned his head slightly to see Blaine Baxter crouched in the trees, his rifle pointed at the group below. Sheriff Poole couldn't get any men for them, and the trio had spent the night tracking the group, not willing to wait for morning's light with the vague promise that maybe men would join them then. The final decision to move ahead with bets on the river had been Jack's idea. Benjamin had learned a long time before to trust Jack's instincts completely.

"Wait until they are in the center. They won't risk entering until they are over there where there's more rock. It's more cover and better footing to try and cross." Jack bit down on his inner cheek as he watched a man he hadn't seen before lift Piper up to Charles Dewitt. He wrapped his arms loosely around her as he regathered his reins and sent his horse into the water.

Benjamin steadied his gun, waiting for Jack's command. He may have been the ranking officer, but Jack was truly the one in charge, and he didn't despise it one bit. Jack had this work in his blood. He was meant to do it.

"Alright," Jack breathed. "Last horse is in the water. Let them get a little closer." He raised his hand beside his ear, and Blaine Brackett emerged from the shadow of the trees, his legs still bent and head low. Jack watched as Charles's horse staggered as the water grew deeper, but it kept going at a slow, steady pace. Soon the horse would be practically swimming. Jack held his breath as Charles's horse came closer to the water's edge on their side. His head moved, a low growl escaping his lips as two horses came forward and passed Charles and Piper. Jack aimed and shot the man on the lead horse, quickly cocking the hammer again and shooting the one directly beside him.

Charles's head shot upward and scanned the rock ahead, his lips moving quickly calling out orders to the others. He slapped the reins against his horse's neck, trying to hurry the horse along. Piper gripped him, her eyes large as the horse struggled to gain footing, her head angled downward at the bodies floating in the water, blood darkening the water around and under their heads.

"Let's go!" Jack yelled and scrambled to his feet. They needed to reach the bottom to get Piper before Charles could get away with her. Blaine stayed at the top and began picking off the members of the gang who were foolish enough to keep pushing forward. Jack watched with a quick flick of his eyes as another one of Charles's men dropped from his horse.

Jack and Benjamin took the narrow pathway from the rock area back down to the water's edge. Their horses were hidden amongst the trees. Jack and Benjamin's feet hit the ground as Charles and Piper burst through the underbrush on Charles's horse. Jack yelped in pain as he lost his footing and rolled the final few feet to the bottom, a jagged piece of rock tearing through fabric and flesh. He hissed and jumped into his saddle, yanking at the tied reins to free them from their loose knot. His own pain fading as he focused on the retreating hindquarters of the horse that held Piper.

Benjamin lowered himself to a crouch and fired his gun as one of the gang tried to follow. Another shot echoed from above them where Blaine was still positioned. Jack did some quick math. Four were down, and one was ahead of him. That left five more who would either follow or who would run in the opposite direction.

Jack held his gun tightly in his hand, hoping for a clean shot at Charles. He could have screamed for joy when he saw the trees thinning ahead of him indicating a clearing was ahead. Charles was driving his horse hard, and Jack was sure Piper would either be thrown or would hit her head and die. Leftover leaves from the previous fall flew into the air in the wake of the horse's hooves.

Jack pulled back hard on the reins of his horse as Charles's horse cleared the trees and underbrush. The animal let out a scream of pain and fear. Charles's horse had hit a hole and his legs twisted, sending it to the ground in a sickening swift movement.

Jack watched in horror as he dismounted. Piper was thrown, and her body rolled and tumbled several feet before coming to a face down stop. For a moment she didn't move a muscle. Charles landed nearby and scrambled his way to Piper, yanking her upward, and placing a strong arm over her throat. His other hand pushed the barrel of his gun to her head. Piper blinked, her body wanting to sag as she fought for consciousness. One sleeve of her dress hung loosely around her elbow, having been torn from the fall. Jack winced inwardly as he watched blood drip from her forehead.

"Let her go, Dewitt! You have nowhere to run to!"

"There's always somewhere to run to!" His green eyes were completely round and frantic. His head jerked, but he kept his eyes on Jack as more gunfire sounded in the distance. Jack imagined he was doing the math too, counting who might be left in his dwindling gang.

"Your gang is being picked apart, Charles. You don't have help coming. Let Piper go!"

Piper swallowed. "Do what he says, Charles. He'll kill you," she whispered, keeping her eyes on Jack.

"Shut up!" Charles yelled pressing the gun tighter against her head. Piper whimpered and closed her eyes.

"Last chance, Dewitt," Jack said. The gun tilted as Charles pushed it against Piper's head and he began to back away. His horse had righted himself and was hobbling towards his owner, soft neighing calling out for help. The movement of Charles's hand gave Jack all the information he needed. Charles had forgotten to pull the hammer back on his pistol.

Jack looked at Piper's silently moving lips as he moved his gun a hair to one side and shot Charles in the elbow of the arm that held the gun to Piper's precious head. Charles's arm flew backward, sending the gun sailing away from him, as he reached to cradle his arm. He was bent at the waist and was still trying to back away.

"Not another step or this one will take out your knee."

As if to protect his knee caps, Charles fell to the ground with a low wail escaping his lips. Footsteps crashed through the brush behind him, but Jack didn't look. He kept his eyes on Charles. Benjamin darted forward and descended on Charles, a rope for his hands at the ready. Blaine was close behind him and took hold of Charles's horse.

"We got two more, but the others went back across the river and scattered like little mice."

"Good work, Blaine thank you," Jack said and holstered his gun, moving his long legs simultaneously in long strides to Piper. She opened her mouth and fell forward into his arms.

"I'm so sorry!" she sobbed. "I'm so sorry! Please forgive me!"

"There's nothing to forgive, Piper," Jack murmured into her tangled hair. "I understand."

She jerked her tear stained face upwards.

"No. No, you don't. I was ate up with pride and anger. They're both sins. I didn't give you a fair chance."

Jack helped her to the ground and shook his head.

"I made myself a promise Piper, that I would give you whatever you wanted once I got you back. I'll put you on a ship back to England if you want. If you want to stay here in America, I'll help you get settled somewhere more to your liking. I'll take you back to Boston even. I just wanted you to be alright."

Piper's eyes searched his face. "I want you, Jack. I want to be with you."

Jack closed his eyes, and a burst of air escaped his lips.

"You want to be with me?"

Piper nodded. "I'm sorry it took me being kidnapped to see that God had handpicked you for me. I'm sorry it took that for me to appreciate you."

"I love you, Piper," Jack said and lowered his lips to hers.

Piper accepted his kiss, not caring about his beard or his long hair. She didn't care anymore about his rough ways. She only felt a love blossom in her chest for him, and that was all that mattered. It was a love that didn't need social boundaries or genealogical ties. It didn't need fine things or big houses. He was the man God had picked for her. She knew it as well as she knew her name.

"We don't have time for that!" Benjamin laughed. "We need to round up those loose horses. Charlie boy has informed me that most of the money was dispersed in the saddle bags." He grinned down at the then openly crying Charles Dewitt. "We stand a good chance of getting most of the people's money back."

"Can you walk?" Jack asked Piper, helping her up gently from the ground.

"I think so."

"I'll put you on my horse. I can handle two leads at once."

"Whatever you say," Piper gratefully breathed with a wide smile on her face.

Jack stared in amazement at his bride to be. Drying tears had left streaks through the days' worth of dirt on her face, and her dress was ripped in places and dirty as well. Her hair was no longer pinned up, and in places was desperately tangled. Yet, she was the most beautiful thing he had ever seen.

Piper waited patiently sitting sideways on Jack's horse as she watched the men quickly gather up the remaining horses. Only one seemed skittish and required them to chase it.

"These horses will bring a good amount of money to offset whatever the caravan lost from the robbery."

"They sure will," Blaine agreed with Benjamin. Both men looked to Jack for his opinion on the matter, but he only had eyes for Piper as he mounted his horse and began speaking softly to her. Benjamin nudged Blaine Brackett, his heart swelling within his chest for his friend. Yes, Black Hands had fallen in love after all, and it looked like she had finally come to her senses too.

"Oh, Charlie boy," Benjamin play punched Charles Dewitt's thigh as he double checked his hand ties. "We have a bit of a bumpy road ahead, so hang on." Benjamin laughed aloud and mounted his gelding as he reached for the reins to the horse Charles sat upon, yet had no control over. He was too busy moaning every few seconds, the tightly tied bandana around his upper arm only served to stifle the blood flow, but did nothing for the pain.

Benjamin couldn't help but laugh more and continue his teasing as the party began its trip back to town. Blaine had expertly tied together the horses they had gathered, still saddled, and led them along in an obedient little row.

216

"Keep your eyes open," Jack warned. "We don't need an ambush for those saddle bags."

"We got it. Just tend to your woman," Benjamin said and looked at Charles with a raised eyebrow. "That is his woman, you know that now, right?"

Charles groaned and rolled his head back along his shoulders.

"Sure you do!" Benjamin chortled.

They began their slow journey back to town, and before Jack knew it, Piper was sound asleep, her head resting on his chest. It was the most peaceful moment he had known for months; maybe ever.

God, I don't know if you hear men like me, but I thank you for bringing Piper back to me. I hear you don't make bargains, but I swear that I will go to church with her. Any church she wants as long as she stays with me for the rest of my life.

The day was nearly finished when the ragamuffin group entered the town. Sheriff Poole and Deputy Rodgers were more than happy to take Charles to the doctor and then back to the jailhouse once the doctor patched him up as best he could. It was the best news they could hear that Charles Dewitt would never use that arm or hand to shoot a gun again.

"Look what else I found out." Sheriff Poole grinned and handed Jack a wanted poster. He tapped the edge with a finger. "Look familiar?"

Jack studied the picture and nodded. "It's Charles Dewitt with a mustache."

"Charles Mackenzie," he corrected. "He's wanted in Ohio for armed robbery and murder."

"As part of the Faceless Gang," Jack said flatly.

"According to Charlie Boy, the Faceless Gang took him in once they found out he was going to rob our caravan. They were working their way up to him when that train robbery happened a few weeks ago. Apparently, they had planned this for more than three months," Benjamin explained. "He had become their new leader."

219

"Not a very good one," Deputy Rodgers snickered.

"No indeed," Benjamin agreed.

Jack rose slowly from the chair he was seated in.

"I need to get back over to the doctor's and see if Piper is done."

"Looks like you need to clean yourself up as well."

Jack looked down at his torn shirt and vest. The jagged cut from his fall had dried blood caked around it, and every move reminded him of the new injury.

"Let the doctor look at it," Benjamin warned.

"I'll do that." Jack smiled and left the Sheriff's office, missing the comments as he went.

"He's like an entirely different man," Sheriff Poole said in wonder.

"He's in love."

Jack walked with a new sense of purpose to the doctor's building. Piper had minor cuts and bruising, and the doctor was going to see about her still sprained ankle. It was a miracle nothing worse had happened to her. He lifted his eyes to the quickly disappearing sun.

Thank you, God. Thank you.

Jack nodded his head to Bonnie and Mrs. Brackett. Baby Ruth wasn't present for a change, and Bonnie held Mrs. Baxter's hand firmly in her own, patting it in a steady, gentle rhythm.

"Where's your baby, Bonnie?"

"Blaine took her and the boys. We're just waiting to see Piper."

"Is she hurt badly?" Mrs. Baxter's eyes came up, still watery. Jack imagined they would be watery for a long time.

"Nothing life threatening." He smiled. "Just minor stuff."

"That's good."

Jack entered the doctor's building and went straight to the back room. He knocked on the partially opened door.

"Come in." The doctor had a bored nasally voice, but his face was round and inviting. "Hello, Marshall," he said as Jack stuck his head in the door. "Your little lady will be just fine. She needs to stay off her foot for a couple days though."

"I'll make sure she does. I'll serve her food in bed if need be."

"She can walk back to the hotel, but I want her to rest at least two days before continuing on with the caravan."

"Yes. That's fine." Jack smiled crookedly at Piper. Two days to rest. Two days to see about a minister. Marrying her before Detroit would be a good thing. It would ensure no other people could change her mind about him. Jack cleared his throat. "I took a tumble while we were out." He pointed to his side. "A rock ripped me a little bit."

Piper inhaled sharply. "A little bit? Looks like it gouged you!"

"Yes, well…it did a little."

The doctor shook his head and chuckled.

"Have a seat in that chair there and let's have a look."

Jack took Piper's hand in his as they walked slowly to his horse to get the saddle bags and head up to the room Bonnie had gotten for Piper. She had made arrangements for herself, baby Ruth, and Mrs. Baxter to stay with Piper, while Jack and Blaine would share a room with the boys. He would have rather hung twine and a blanket again, but he supposed the lack of temptation would be a good thing. The kiss after she had been rescued had stirred something deep within him.

"How would you feel about finding a minister here and getting married before we have to leave?"

Piper thought about it for a moment, a smile spreading across her face.

"I would love that," she blushed profusely. "Maybe we can share a room as husband and wife our last night here."

Jack grinned, and for once he blushed as well.

"I can talk to Sheriff Poole about the license. I'll do it first thing in the morning."

"Good." Piper breathed in deeply, the weariness of the past two days leaking from her like a dripping rag. "I'll sleep well tonight, I think."

"Me too. I just need to meet with the men and let them know that we can't leave until the day after tomorrow. But for now…I would like for you to have something to take to your room."

"What is it?"

Jack stopped at his horse and took the saddle and saddle bags from the horse's back before leaving the things at Piper's feet and leading the horse to the communal barn for the hotel. He gladly gave a stable boy a half dollar to tend to the horse. The young man's grin told him that he had overpaid by a lot, but to Jack, it was worth it. Maybe he was feeding the boy's family for the week with the money.

Jack came back to Piper and opened one of the flaps on the saddle bag. He pulled a small stack of worn papers out and handed them to her.

"What are these?"

Jack pressed his lips together.

"I didn't want you to think I'm just a mindless brute. You know…lacking culture."

"Jack…"

"No, it's fine. I just want you to read a few of these. I've been writing them since I was twenty. I save the ones I like the best. They are poems."

Piper's eyes enlarged as she looked at the papers in her hands, the script a tight, neat writing. The profound feeling that she was about to take a peek into his soul was overwhelming.

"May I give you something to read too?"

"Sure."

They worked their way up to the rooms. Bonnie and Mrs. Brackett had already gotten

228

Piper her dinner, and it waited by the turned down bed on a tray. Luckily the room had two beds. It was meant for a larger family.

Jack waited with his head down as Piper gathered Mrs. Baxter to her, her mouth uttering soft words and quoted bible verses about faith and strength.

Mrs. Baxter pulled away gently as her tears subsided.

"Thank you, dear. Thank you."

"What will you do now?"

Mrs. Baxter shrugged slowly. "I really don't know. I don't want to go back to Boston without him. I guess I'll just keep going to Detroit."

Piper looked over her shoulder at Jack for a moment before returning her face to Mrs. Baxter. She smiled softly.

"We'll help you figure something out." She moved away and once again was grateful how Bonnie and Mrs. Baxter had taken care of everything for her, right down to having her things brought up from the wagon. She opened her carpetbag and pulled her Bible out. She limped back to Jack and handed it to him.

"I know you aren't fond of this, but it means so much to me. Would you please read a little tonight?"

Jack nodded and reverently took the worn book from her hands.

"Go on now and get settled." He smiled and kissed her cheek, ignoring the pain lacing up his rib cage as he bent towards her. He straightened and saw the other women had their heads together and were whispering. That time it wasn't the work of busybodies; it was just the knowing words of two women who had already known first love and the joyous heart pattering that it could bring.

"See you tomorrow." Piper smiled.

Jack nodded and left the room, quietly closing the door behind himself.

Piper sat up reading the papers over and over again. There was twenty pages total, and she loved them all, but there was one that she loved the most. She glanced at the bed where the sleeping forms of Bonnie and Mrs. Baxter laid back to back, and little Ruth curled against her mother's side. She turned back to the poem, vowing to read it just one more time.

I rush into the world to bring back the ones trying to destroy it.

I feel the heat of my duties like amber fire in my blood, but I'm not satisfied.

I long for something more.

I long for someone more.

I see my days not stretching with joy.

I see my days cut short from grief.

I will mourn the empty places of my heart, and the empty spot of my bed, until you come.

If you come. If only you would come.

Piper felt her eyes prick at the simplistic, yet emotionally raw poem. She stacked the papers neatly and set them on the other pillow that she was not going to use. She felt comforted knowing they were near. They were Jack's words. His heart and soul poured out onto thin paper.

If you come. If only you would come.

Piper blew out the candle on the bedside table and laid on her side.

"I'm here, Jack. I'm here to fill your empty places."

Chapter Ten

The morning was a bustle of activity.
Jack did as he had told Piper he would and
took care of talking to Sheriff Poole and had
visited the town minister, even though he had
only slept a few hours after having stayed
awake most of the night reading Piper's
Bible. He had never taken the time to read
much in the Bible, and it was like nothing he
had ever read before. He made it through
the entire book of Genesis and had skipped
forward and read the book of Matthew too.
He couldn't wait to read more. He couldn't
wait to know more. He had gone to his knees
in the middle of the night and told Jesus that

he was a sinner. He had thanked him for dying on that cross. He had thanked him for his meddling father having a hand in bringing Piper to him. The morning had looked new and different. Maybe it was the sudden peace in his heart. Peace that he hadn't known before.

"They're about ready," Benjamin said as he stuck his head in the door.

"Does this look alright? It's my last vest and shirt," Jack said with a sigh and a slight frown.

Benjamin entered the room with a laugh. "You look fine, Marshall, but I don't think you need the badge on while you're getting hitched."

"No, I do. It's part of me. The 'me' of right now, anyway."

Benjamin nodded his understanding.

"Then you best leave it." He winked. "So, I caught a glimpse of your bride in her borrowed dress. That takes care of the old and the borrowed, and it looks like the new is going to be you, but I don't know about the blue part."

"We don't need superstition."

"Then let's go, handsome. The pastor won't wait forever."

Jack and Benjamin left the inn and hurried to the little church that sat on the outskirts of the town. It was a plain white building of clapboard, but at the moment it looked like the grandest building ever to Jack.

He couldn't stop grinning, and it only grew as he entered the church and saw that the entire caravan was in attendance.

Bonnie hurried towards him with a smile, her red hair coming unpinned as usual.

"I have her hidden out back! Go on up front!" She practically ran past him and out the front doors of the church, her skirts swishing as she went.

Jack nodded to the minister, offering his thanks again. The man smiled happily reiterating that he was more than happy to accommodate two people in love.

"Especially when one just turned their life over to the Lord less than twenty-four hours ago," he whispered.

A hush went over the church as Bonnie began marching up the center aisle, the church piano playing a hymn at the command of Mrs. Baxter's hands. Everyone stood, and Jack froze as Piper stepped through the church doorway, her hand resting in the crook of Blaine Brackett's elbow. The dress was a simple white thing with a veil fastened at the crown of her head that hung down her back. It was looser than what she needed but had been cinched at the waist with a broad satin ribbon of blue.

"Looks like she got the blue after all," Benjamin whispered.

Jack didn't seem to hear anything as Piper came closer. Her limping gait was even slower than the normal Bride's March, and he just wanted to jump over alter, sweep her into his arms, and run back with her, just to speed things up.

Jack couldn't take his eyes off Piper as the minister talked about love and unions before finally coming to the vows. The words 'You may now kiss your bride' were barely from the minister's lips before Jack had Piper pulled tightly to him and tasted the sweetness of her mouth. His head reeled as the caravan's people cheered and clapped. All he could think about was how he would taste her lips for the rest of his life. He would have a wife until death did they part, and finally, Black Hands Jack Walker would never be lonely again.

THE END

Word-of-mouth is crucial for any author to succeed. If you enjoyed the book, please take the time to leave a review on Amazon. Even if it's just a sentence or two. It would make all the difference and would be very much appreciated.

Want a FREE copy of one of my Western Short Stories? Click the sign-up link below to join my Exclusive Reader's List. After signing up, you will receive your FREE copy of "Fools Rush In".

Sign up for my Exclusive Reader's List by entering the following link into your internet browser: http://eepurl.com/cvmjAv

Visit Eveline Hart's Facebook fan page at the link below:

https://www.facebook.com/Eveline-Hart-342789062723747

About Author – Eveline Hart

First and foremost, I am the mother of a handsome two-year-old boy. He is my pride and joy. We currently reside in a small beach town in the South. I have always loved writing, but until recently, never considered writing books. Just recently, I've decided to try it out, and I hope you enjoy reading these books just as much as I've enjoyed writing them. Thank you for taking the time to read my books.

Author's Note

This is the third Western novella I've written. I just want to say, as an up and coming author, I don't have the funds to pay for a good editor or cover designer, so please excuse any mistakes you may find. I plan to write more books in this series, especially if I hear from you the readers that you want more. Please either join my Exclusive Reader's List or engage on my Facebook page to let me know if you want me to write more books for you to read. Do you have ideas, themes or topics you'd like me to write about? If so, let's hear it!

Sign up for my Exclusive Reader's List by entering the following link into your internet browser: http://eepurl.com/cvmjAv

Visit Eveline Hart's Facebook fan page here:

https://www.facebook.com/Eveline-Hart-342789062723747

Made in the USA
Columbia, SC
25 January 2018